Eating My Words

A collection of flash-fictions

Edited by
Calum Kerr, Angela Readman
and Amy Mackelden

A National Flash-Fiction Day and Gumbo Press publication

First Published 2014 by National Flash-Fiction Day
in association with Gumbo Press

National Flash-Fiction Day
18 Caxton Avenue
Bitterne
Southampton
SO19 5LJ
www.nationalflashfictionday.co.uk

A CIP Catalogue record for this book
is available from the British Library

ISBN 978-1500110871

For Flash-Fictioneers everywhere

Contents

Micro-fiction Winners

Foreword

One issue we have, when we open submissions for our anthologies, is how to pick the theme for the stories. There is always a worry that it might be too wide - so the stories don't come together to make a coherent collection - or too narrow - so writers either find it too hard to come up with something which fits, or they all end writing about the same ideas.

This year our theme was 'The Senses' and we made the point that this could cover not just the standard five senses, or even what is referred to as the 'sixth' sense, but also a sense of fun, or foreboding, or even fair play.

Of course we needn't have worried about our choice of theme, and as the stories you are about to read will attest, flash-fiction writers all over the world responded with imagination, empathy and wit to create an anthology to which we are more than proud to put our names.

The task of choosing was, as ever, a difficult one, and there were many stories which we liked but didn't have the space for. Occasionally, we found ourselves looking at stories on similar subjects, and had to make difficult decisions to keep the balance in the anthology right. What follows are the very best stories received, and the ones which come together to create a collection which can be seen as a single piece of work.

At the end of the book you will also find the ten stories which topped this year's micro-fiction competition. There was no theme for that, just the limit of 100 words, and these are the best stories out of almost 400 received. Quite an achievement, and a fine selection.

Congratulations to all who were successful in making it into this anthology which, we feel, stands well alongside our previous books: *Jawbreakers* and *Scraps*. We have enjoyed putting this selection together, and we are sure that you will enjoy reading it.

As ever, don't forget that this collection is part of the annual National Flash-Fiction Day, occurring in 2014 on 21st June. There are many events going on to celebrate the day, and all the details can be found on our website at www.nationalflashfictionday.co.uk.

But, for now, just sit back and eat up the words to come. We're sure they'll excite your palate.

Calum Kerr & Angela Readman
Editors
June 2014

One Rat for Every Person
Becky Tipper

On the news that morning, I'd heard a report about how there were sixty million rats in Britain. That's one for every person, they said. So I wasn't surprised when I saw one on my way to work, scuttling between the bins behind Asda. And when he hopped on the bus and sat next to me – glancing around with his beady eyes, his whiskers trembling – I felt pleased that we'd found each other, out of the sixty million.

At work, he picked things up easily and got along with everyone. In fact, they called that evening to say that I needn't come back since he was doing such a good job. (My boss, who I'd never liked anyway, added shirtily that I should seriously reflect on whether I considered myself personable enough to pursue a career in customer services.) With nothing to do the next day, I went to the pub. Around eight, I was about to head back when my girlfriend phoned to say that I needn't bother coming home. Since I was so late, they had ordered a pizza and were watching *Sex and the City*. The rat was better company, she said, and less domineering about the TV.

I spent the night behind Asda. It was more comfortable than you might think. I hadn't eaten all day but there was plenty of food that was only slightly out-of-date, or the packaging a bit crumpled. I found some onion bhajis and an egg mayonnaise sandwich, which tasted just as good as usual, better even – there in the rich dark air of the city, under the strip of stars between the buildings. I slept well, soothed by the hum of the machines constantly cooling and heating and circulating like internal organs. In the morning, when I woke, I felt like a new person.

You adapt to life's little changes, don't you? And mostly, when you look back you can see they were for the best anyway. It's been years now and I rarely think about my former life, although from time to time I catch a scent in the air that fills me with longing, and I'll go and visit my old flat. I'll scrabble up the drainpipe and perch on the windowsill where I can see into the living room. They'll be sitting together on the couch as he nibbles crumbs of cheese from her hand, or she'll be petting him absent-mindedly while they watch a film. I see her hand slide over his grey fur and rest on his long fleshy tail, and for a moment I'll wish it was me. I imagine myself there, nuzzling her palm, and I think how I wouldn't even care what we watched on TV. But then I hear the neighbours trundling their bins out, and the darkness feels sleek and cool on my back, and the millions of stars that pierce the sky are so fresh and alive, and I turn and slide back into the night.

Taste

Adam J Wolstenholme

She knew she had no taste because her boyfriend told her so. It started on their first date in the union bar, in 1997, when Wannabe by the Spice Girls came on the jukebox. She felt happy and excited to be with him, and without realising, began grinning and swaying in her seat.

Connor cringed. "Tell me you don't like this."

"It's fun."

"You've got no taste."

He was smiling, so it didn't seem serious then.

Over the next few months she decided she'd never met anyone so sure of themselves, and she was delighted when he suggested they move in together.

He got very drunk that first night, and she woke early and read for an hour. He stirred and squinted up at her.

"John Updike, eh?"

"It's great," she said, without thinking.

"Updike is McCartney," said Connor, turning over, "to Saul Bellow's Lennon."

How could she tell him that she'd always preferred McCartney's songs? Or that when her Dad died, when she was 15, Yesterday had given her a life-saving assurance that she was not alone?

After they graduated she found a job at an insurance company while Connor worked on his PhD. In that first year she learned a lot from him. She learned that what she liked and what was good were not the same thing. She still bought novels, but read them when he wasn't around. And usually he drove, and played his own CDs. Hers were left out of their cases, became scratched, forgotten in the depths of the glove compartment.

Connor failed his PhD around the same time that she was promoted. Given that he didn't have to be up in the mornings – and that they were also supposed to be trying for a baby - it was natural that she did most of the evening driving. But still Connor chose the music.

Driving home from a party – at which he'd held forth on the badness of the government, America and Coldplay – she put on the latest Stones album.

"Oh, not this! They should've stopped after Sticky Fingers. They're such parodies of themselves."

"But it rocks. Surely you like what you like."

He looked affronted. "You've got a lot to learn." He removed the Stones, rummaged clumsily in the glove compartment and rammed in a CD: The car was filled with cold, metallic bleeping. When she was sure he was asleep she snapped the music off. She stopped at the lights, looked at him snoring, at the string of saliva running down the greying stubble on his double chin. As she drove on she felt a terrible decision coursing through her limbs and stepped hard on the accelerator.

On her fortieth birthday, the DJ played YMCA. She danced alone, laughing, marvelling at how something so shit could make her feel so good. If she closed her eyes, and stood very close to the distorting speakers, it was almost loud enough to drown out the voice of Connor, the arbiter of taste.

Tasty

Andy Cashmore

He starts his laptop and like clockwork opens an incognito tab. His hands tremble as the search bar flashes impatiently. He types the first letter of the four, 'p', and pauses like an adventurer at the point of no return. He inputs the remaining three letters incorrectly as 'ron' but hits enter anyway. Some unusual sites appear that are close to what he wants, but he fears they harbour viruses.

He corrects his spelling and finds his staple means of nourishment. Thumbnails line up in even columns. His stomach fizzes like a soda pop when he sees the pictures of women dressed in various levels of clothing. One of the women has her mouth filled with a thick sausage, another is on her back by a man wearing a chef's uniform, there's one set in a public restaurant.

But these are all tame to his needs. He goes to the categories and picks out his fetish. When the page loads, one thumbnail stands out: a portrait of a woman with a white dribble on her lips. He lowers his hand underneath his clothes and clicks. The video begins with a woman lying on a table, legs in the air. In front of her is a loaf of bread, lettuce, tomato and chicken, the latter which turns him off, being a vegetarian. This isn't what he was expecting. Still, time is limited so he strokes his belly and feels the first sensations of hunger trickle away.

The woman takes a knife and chops the tomato with a firm, jerking movement. He imitates it on the curls of his treasure trail. His stomach gets smaller at the sight of the chicken but it isn't on screen for long. When the lettuce is washed his stomach swells again. Then the woman giggles and pulls a large tub of mayonnaise into shot. This is it. He rubs harder. Pop goes the lid. She sticks a knife into the tub. He rubs harder, making a lot of noise as the white substance drips from the knife. The woman lets it hang just above her head and opens up like a piranha. His stomach cramps: he knows there's still the sandwich but this is his favourite part. The mayonnaise droops, suspended in the air. He writhes in his chair. Finally it falls and splashes on the corner of her mouth. The woman makes an agreeable moan like it's the tastiest thing she's ever eaten. His stomach kicks as ecstasy rushes up his digestive tract, and leaves through his mouth as a loud burp.

The front door closes. He replaces the porn window with a word document and pulls his shirt over his belly. His girlfriend comes upstairs and jumps into his lap. She whispers in his ear that she's *really* hungry and is going to cook them something tasty. She bites his ear and skips away. He hears a pan sizzling and it makes him feel sick: he worries he won't be able to finish.

Fear

Moira Conway

"The wind the wind the wind blows higher
  In comes Eileen from the skyer"
The girls skipped into the rope till everyone's name had
been called, then the rhyme went into reverse.
  "The wind the wind the wind blows higher
  Out goes Eileen from the skyer."
As the girls played Tom crept up behind them, then he
pounced!
  "Look what I'VE GOT!"
He thrust a cockroach in Eileen's face. She screamed and
ran away, the others looked, then they screamed and ran
away. Molly hid behind a tree. He wandered off grinning.
The girls ran in to tell Eileen's Mam, who said she would
have a word with his mother. Molly wasn't sure that would
do a lot of good, they were a queer family. For the rest of
the day they played in Eileen's back garden. When Molly
knew her tea would be ready she set off for home. As she
walked up the street she saw Tom leaning against the wall.
What would she do if he had the cockroach? He might put
it in her hair! It might crawl in her ear! As she grew nearer
he stepped forward.
  "Look what I've got!"
She steeled herself. Her ears were thumping, her flesh
creeping. He opened his hand to show her the cockroach.
Against all her instincts she moved towards him.
  "Do you like him?"
She clenched her fists behind her back. Her mouth was
dry, her throat tight.
  "Yeh! Where did you get it?"
  "On holiday in Scotland."

"We've been to Scotland."

His face relaxed he started to smile.

"We go camping there every summer. There are adders and grass snakes and slow worms and all sorts. I bring them back and keep them in my bedroom"

The hair stood up on the back of Molly's neck. IN HIS BEDROOM! The cockroach was crawling over his hand waving its wavy bits at her menacingly like a monster from a horror movie.

"Would you like a hold."

THINK QUICK MOLLY!

"I might drop him."

Mrs Wardropper was surprised to see her son Tom go through the kitchen with Molly. He didn't normally get on with other children, especially girls. She was pleased.

"Just showing Molly my snakes Mam."

She didn't notice Molly's clenched fists and pale face as she followed Tom slowly up the stairs. Along one wall of his bedroom was a row of aquariums with lids on the top but no water. Tom took the lid off one and put the cockroach back in. There were lots of them in there it looked a horror film. Tom took the lid off another and took out a small snake. The markings were subtle shades of green and brown, she felt an urge to touch it.

"What does it feel like?" She thought it would be wet and slimy.

"Do you want to hold it?"

Gathering up all of the courage she could muster, she unclenched her fists and held out her hands to take the snake.

Lear Bus

John F King

Some fool had left King Lear on the bus.

I opened the pages at random. He was right about regret. I was too old to repeat mistakes now too. All that past.

I'm sitting on the top deck. Number 14 as you ask. Some time since I've been on a bus. Anywhere. I've missed them. I know I ought to look out of the window as we cross the river, urban delta, spreading in all directions. The line spoke to me '…that way madness lies.'

When I looked up the river was behind me. Still it came flooding back, I should have known the difference - a sense of ending or a clarificatory row that would have allowed our journey to continue. Spring would have seen us home.

If pushed I'd say it was when you started your new year fitness regime that it started to go wrong. Leaping off the bus three stops earlier you seemed so resolute. It was a 12 – if memory serves – right side of the bridge.

You responded to my 'I'll love you until the end of time' with

'That's not long enough,' I was hedging with finites, speaking in lines.

As the bus drew away you said it seems nearer the end than the beginning.

I said ' stop this right now, do you know what you are doing?'

Eventually you reduced the number of stops so much you weren't getting on the bus at all.

Only after you'd gone I realized I could never have hoped to keep up.

I left Lear in the terminus. The bus reversed out for the

return journey. I was looking at the route map before I felt the river behind me again.

Ought. Should. Would. Could.

Hey, Why Not Be a Daughter?
Angela Readman

If you see your father on a bridge, what do you do? He's alone. He could jump. His hair is a silver web around his cap. He looks down at a paper boat. The river drags it this way and that.

You consider him carefully, buttons on his cuffs pinging the metal railings. You have an inkling you've seen him before. He has this clockwork walk as if someone wound him up a long time ago. You know that walk. You walk the same, walk until your feet are persuaded to stay put.

Don't stare. Of course, he's not your father, probably, but he could be. His age is a wrinkled suit. It fits. You inspect the dismantled origami of his face and feel he used to smile a lot, all the lines are there. You could crack a joke and pop that smile into place. You'd say, 'Hey, let's make another paper boat. Let's race.' And there you'd be, in November, boating with your father.

You wonder if he has a daughter. It's doubtful. You'd think she'd iron his shirt. Or, perhaps he does. Perhaps she'll always have pigtails, a small face at a hazy window imprinted to his mind like a condom circle in a leather wallet. Or, she moved, probably to New Zealand. In any case, she's not here now.

The wind whispers snow's around the corner. Winter will make walking slippery, sentence the man indoors, if he has a house at all. It could be different. You could link his arm, lead him home, buy turkey. You hate ironing, but you suppose you could learn. You'd scorch stuff. He'd curse then laugh. Every time you get the iron out, he'll shout to his shirts like a sergeant instructing a line of anaemic men, 'Look out Lads! Here she comes!' There'll be nothing for it but sweaters you'll knit that will make his arms itch. He'll scratch and say, 'My daughter made this.' And he'll put up with it, being itchy, the itch is love.

The paper boat snares on Styrofoam under the bridge. The man looks to pigeons on the path. You wish you had pockets bursting with bread. If this was a story, a lady carrying toilet paper would exit a bush and return to the man, or, a boy with a ball would bounce up, but he doesn't. It's just you, a man and no stories crossing the bridge, chapstick sealing the words on your lips. 'Are you a father? I could be a daughter, just for Christmas perhaps.' He'd look you over and sense you have something to give. There's a vacancy you feel in his eyes as you lower yours, afraid of what they may advertise. You walk on and look back at a flap of pigeons flying off all at once. How do they know? The man's eyes lift to the sky with you, look at scattering wings.

A Bottle of Silence

Sal Page

While they were out, I filled a big bottle with beautiful quiet, sweeping it through the emptiness, collecting the silence and stillness and sealing it within.

They're back. The radio is blaring and thumping. He's droning on about nothing. She's hoovering. The dog is barking. Now they're stomping around. There's an argument brewing. An argument I'll get sucked into, hearing things I don't want to know about.

So when it gets too much to bear I'll open the bottle with a pop of the stopper. I'll stand in the centre of the room, tipping the bottle slightly as the smooth delicious silence pours out. Released, it'll fill the room from floor to ceiling; flowing and curling gradually into each of the four corners. The quietness will wrap itself around their noise, stifling it and squeezing it into nothingness. Then a ringing silence will hang in the air for hours, so rich and warm I'll actually be able to taste it.

The Sundial

Rhys Barter

Sitting alone in London's crowded Soho Square, Holly opened her book to the page she had marked only hours earlier with an impromptu folded corner, and forced herself to read.

Immediately she was distracted as the corner began fluttering in the wind. For as long as she'd been reading her parents had drummed into her that books were not to have their corners folded, and that to do so was tantamount to vandalism; an unacceptable act, when anything, from a receipt to a Post-It note, could serve as a bookmark. Then again, her mother was a librarian, so she was biased.

But why had she folded down the corner before fleeing her flat? It was something she'd never done before, and she felt an overwhelming sense of guilt at having defaced the book. As if mirroring her feelings, the corner itself bowed its head in shame.

She had nothing to feel guilty about, however. The argument that had forced her out on to the street may have been brutal, but it hadn't been her fault. Her bookmark had presumably been amongst the sheaf of papers that, in anger, she had launched across the room. It stood to reason that she would've folded down the corner so as not to lose her place.

No, that theory didn't make any sense at all. She hated people who folded corners. She hated herself for having done it.

So *why* had she done it? Had her fury temporarily relieved her of her senses? Had she felt the need to combat her own hurt by destroying something she loved?

Today, a folded page, she thought. *Tomorrow, all out biblioclasm.*

So what now? She had stormed outside with nothing except her book. Eventually she would need to return in order to fetch her things.

She stared at the page in front of her, trying to decide what to do. Her heart was on the verge of breaking. Should she let it?

God, give me a sign, she thought, and although she had never been particularly religious, she sensed something had changed.

She stared down at the open book in her lap and the shadow of the shameful folded corner caught her eye. It was shaped like an arrow, and it moved across the page like the single, hollow hand of a sundial. And then it seemed to stop. The wind died down and the whole world froze. She read the word the arrow had settled on:

"Forgive."

And then the world lurched back to life. A car backfired, a flock of pigeons took flight, and the sun was obscured by a wandering cloud.

She recalled the inscription on the sundial her parents had kept in the garden when she was a child:

Let others talk of storms and showers, I'll only count your sunny hours.

Methodically, she unfolded the corner of the page and closed her book.

Then she stood up, brushed down her dress, and headed off in the direction of her flat.

Dress Sense

James Coates

The first one is tight, the second and third are too long. The fourth has stitching which digs in and scratches.

"Shall I fetch that first one in a bigger size?" The shop assistant glances at her manicured nails. "Or...not?"

I shake my head.

"You've got to have something Libby." Mum rubs her face. It's thinner than it used to be, paler. The muscles slack.

I look at the floor, and bunch my fists. "I don't want a new dress!"

Mum sighs.

The assistant's lips pinch tight as she looks at the ceiling.

My jumper has holes in both elbows, and one arm is longer than the other. The flaky patch of muted colours on the front, used to be a picture of a cat.

There's a photo at home of Caz wearing the jumper when it was new. The cat is bright eyed and ginger striped. Caz is smiling. She still had hair.

"Libs, we've been through this." Mum crouches next to me, her brown eyes coming level with mine, so that I cannot miss the sheen of restrained tears. "There must be something here. Please? We've been everywhere else."

"I don't want anything." I scuff my foot along the changing room floor. The shop assistant slips away, eyes rolling.

"But, you've grown. Nothing fits, and you can't wear...your sister's clothes forever."

It's been a year. Mum still can't say Caz's name out loud. I'd never complained about the hand-me-downs; it's all I'd ever known. Every toy lovingly tested, her pet rabbit tamed and trained, every item of clothing worn in and made comfortable.

Mum tidies the dresses away, her voice weary. "I thought

24

this blue one looked nice on you." It lingers in her hand a moment before she releases it to the rail.

"Sorry, it's...they didn't feel right. They smell too new, too..." Unworn, unloved? Caz's jumper remembers her shape, remembers the tree climbing, that day on the swings in the rain, the night we went to the restaurant and all the lights went out. It remembers that there used to be laughter, and life.

"But look at the state of that jumper," Mum rubs her face again. "What must people think?" Her eyes harden. "It's got to go."

"No. You can't. Caz's clothes speak to me, they tell a story. Those dresses know nothing. They've done nothing."

"Well, stories or not, you can't wear them any more. They're too small."

"But, I want to be part of their story. Part of something...not...not alone."

Mum bites her lip, and blinks back fresh tears.

On the way to the car we pass a shop with smeared windows. A faded blue teddy and a mannequin wearing a green chequered suit peer out between stacks of puzzles.

"What's that place?"

"Just a charity shop darling, it's full of..." Mum stops, and smiles. "It's full of unfinished stories."

The Working Man's Struggle
Richard Holt

Lad, said Grandpa Reg. There ain't nothing as sure as working men is dealt a bad lot an' have to fight for every scrap or die poor, which is what the bosses want.

I'd heard it before and I knew he'd keep on for maybe two cups of instant til Nan started tutting. Bursting her apron strings. Yes, Dear, she'd say. It'd be all very well if it wasn't so much baloney.

Then Nan would say, Honey, I'll tell you what really happened.

He'd cough out a couple of half sentences in his defence then shuffle out.

Nan would start…Always singing and marching, marching and singing and none of them any good at either. They'd be picketing if the wind blew the wrong way out of the bosses' loos. Him and his mates, marching up and down singing struggle songs like the glorious people's revolution had begun.

Singing so much chances are some feller from Equity would turn up and tell them they needed a ticket for it.

Reg and the Equity bloke would have a punch-up.

Reg would say, no hard feelings. Beer brother? After a couple they'd start singing again and there'd likely be another scrap then more talk about exploiting bosses and not enough smokes.

So they'd have a smoke. Maybe another punch-up or a sing and a march.

Eventually the bosses would get jack of it and call in their goons. Reg would get his nose busted and come home angry about bosses and goons and the bloke from Equity for skiving off from the fight.

Besides, half the time Reg wasn't working or picketing or progressing the cause anyway, unless the cause involved skiving off to race pigeons, while his brave brothers covered for him at the plant.

About when Nan was really firing, Reg would skulk in from the yard and say, are you still goin'?

What if I am? she'd say.

Reg would threaten to withdraw his labour, and she'd say, what labour is that? If anyone strikes around here it'll be me.

Reg would go quiet, then Nan would get him a cuppa and maybe some cake and tell him he could go down the pub later if he didn't get plastered. Talk to your mates about the struggle, she'd say. Tell someone who cares.

You're the only one really cares, he'd say. And she'd give him a big smile.

Nan and Reg battled like that til Nan's heart went. Reg lasted barely another ten months. Went into a home. Faded fast. She used to say he wouldn't work in an iron lung. But she made him work pretty hard for those smiles. It wasn't til Amanda and I were going through a rough patch I realised, thinking about those visits to Nan's, that deep down it was his passion she loved, and that one time, before punch ups and pigeons, it must have been all for her.

Show, Don't Tell

Cathy Bryant

We were both writers, Keiran and I, and we both knew the 'Show Not Tell' rule, so it was obvious what I had to do.

Hey, it's a good rule! Compare the two following descriptions:

1. Caitlin felt very angry and upset. She thought that Kevin was a prick.

2. Caitlin clenched her fists as she felt fury boiling inside her - but she also felt tears begin to prick the backs of her eyes. Kevin is such a big, blind, stupid prick, she thought, her lips thinning with distaste.

See? The second is sooo much better. The reader is right in the action - s/he can actually feel it with the senses, rather than just being given flat information. So I was right to do it, right?

I began by sneering repeatedly at him in public, and making scathing comments. I turned away from him in bed, too, but he just seemed puzzled and sad.

I cranked things up a notch by breaking his precious cat ornament and giving him bad reviews on Amazon. This was serious stuff, and he should have felt the truth with all his being. He did go a bit pale, but he still failed to understand.

I was forced to get extreme and go for the full sensory action thing to convey the information. I invited the postman in - I've always had a thing for him - and fucked him loudly in the living room. Which is beside Keiran's study. Where he was working at the time.

He looked in briefly, made a tearing sound somewhere between a scream and a sigh, and shut the door on the sight.

That night he said, "You don't love me any more. It's over, isn't it, Christine?"

"Yes," I said, pleased that he had finally got it.

Then he said something that proved what a terrible person and writer he was, and why I was right to dump him.

"Why didn't you *tell* me?"

A Sense of Entitlement

E. L. Norry

"Excuse me, do you have a light?"

I stare at the ground. My hands thrust deep in my pockets; my fur collar turned up against the wind and drizzle.

His baritone is rich. "I saw you smoking, earlier. Do you have a light, please? These matches... " he shrugs.

I curl my fingers around the silver lighter inside my pocket. When I hand it to him, he turns it over and reads aloud the inscription. "If there's such a thing as a genius, I am one. If there isn't, I don't care."

"John Lennon." I say, quietly. He holds my gaze a moment too long and I kick the ground.

His expression is quizzical. "I've seen you here before."

I nod. My long hair falls over my face.

"My sister... that's why I'm here," he pauses, and then continues, "I mean, she only died a few months ago..." His voice halts. Just stops dead and I know he doesn't trust himself to speak any further.

I usually stay silent at this point, but I need a new approach; I need to do something radical, something against my instinct in order for this to work. I need to fill this gap; and not with words. I can do this, get this right.

I carefully bring my hand out of my pocket and lay it on his forearm. He looks startled. I deliberately squeeze his forearm, my eyes fixed on his face. His cheeks are flushed and a brown fringe hangs in his eyes. He's in his early forties. Perfect. I lower my chin and peer up through my long eyelashes.

"It's hard." I try to gauge what should come next. "I'm sure she appreciates you coming to visit so often. I know my... " My eyes flicker to the headstone we're in front of. "I know, Bill, my dad... does." I hold my breath.

He takes a deep drag on his cigarette and flicks the ash. His gaze is steady and tone gentle. "You might be right." He leans forward and squints at the headstone. "William Butler. Fell asleep 2002. Much loved. You're always here. Doesn't it get any easier, then?"

"No, it does. It's just for me... there are certain times of the year..." I bite my lip, ease out a tear.

His eyes travel over my body like a laser beam.

No wedding ring; its fate. Damn. Now what? I've tried this routine for months but it's never taken me as far as I'd have liked. A few coffees, one lunch; but I want the real deal. He must be out there somewhere; a gentle malleable man that I can help through his grief, whilst pretending to suffer with mine. Soon he'll realise he's unable to do without me, he'll propose and we'll have children. My happy ending; finally.

He coughs. "It's freezing out here. Have you eaten? Would a spot of lunch be inappropriate?"

There is such a thing as a genius, and I am one.

The Sensation of Pain
Angi Holden

Tom pushed the glasses into a triangle, one between each thumb and forefinger, the third pressed between his index fingers.

'Cheers, mate,' he said, as he lifted the three pints of Tennents in a swift, easy movement and headed back to his friends.

'No, seriously. I read about it in the December journal,' Emma said, shuffling her stool aside to let Tom through. He put the lagers on the table and pushed one towards Jim, another towards Dave.

He picked up his pint and took a deep gulp, allowing the refreshing liquid to wash over his tongue. That's better, he thought. It had been a long shift. Long, tiring and if he was honest, emotional. Although like most nurses, he kept his feelings under wraps.

'What have I missed?' he asked. The girls shuffled up to make space for him on the wooden bench. Jenny rested her hand on his thigh.

'I read about this guy who didn't feel pain,' Emma said.

'Yeah, we've all met those,' quipped Jenny. 'They're called Bastards.' The girls laughed noisily and chinked their glasses of Shiraz in a toast to shared experience.

'Emma was telling us about this article,' said Jim. 'Some kid that was born with no pain reflex. Broke his arm in a fall and didn't realise he'd done any damage. Just carried on. Unbelievable.'

'I don't get it,' said Jenny. 'We see kids in A&E all the time, creased up over nothing more than a sprain.' She turned to Tom. 'You broke your arm, didn't you? How could it not hurt?'

'I dunno. It was a long time ago; I don't remember much. But I guess everyone's got their pain threshold.' Tom reached across the table for the menu. 'Anyone fancy a plate of tortilla chips? I'm starving.'

'The interesting thing was that he trained in medicine,' Emma said, carrying on with her story. It wasn't often that she was the centre of attention, and she wasn't going to be distracted just yet. Not even for a share of tortillas. 'He was poorly a couple of times when he was little and nobody cottoned on till he was really ill.'

'Wow. How scary must that have been for his mum and dad?'

'Exactly. So when he was older he went into nursing. Payback.'

'Chips, definitely chips.' Tom guessed a couple of platters would be enough. He squeezed his way out of the group, counting coins from his pocket. The conversation wafted around him.

'Imagine what his patients would think though? Fancy being given an injection by someone who doesn't know what pain feels like!' Tom noticed Jenny shudder at the thought.

While he waited for the order he watched his friends in the mirror above the bar. He would always be separate. Different. Alone. The platter arrived. Tom took a tortilla from the top and pressed the grilled cheese against the roof of his mouth. The flesh bubbled, without sensation.

This is what pain feels like, he thought.

What I'll Do To Be In Love With You

Simon Sylvester

It took time, and it took trouble, and it cost me everything I had. But after weeks of voodoo, and lightning, and chisels, and harmonic scales, and excruciating pain, the alchemist succeeded.

The alchemist turned me into a harmonica.

I was a boy of flesh and blood. Now I'm made of pear wood, brass and pearl.

I was mute. Now I sing.

You said I was ugly. Now I'm beautiful.

The alchemist delivered me to the stage door, wrapped up in silken ribbons. You cradled me in your rough hands, and then you took me home. You soak my reeds in bourbon, and we kiss every night, and I sleep in your back pocket.

And you're proud of me, now, which is more than I ever managed as your son.

Postcard to my best friend from a non-Londoner, one 'dull... of soul'

Jenny Holden

Outside your flat is where the men of Brixton go to piss. A party in the small hours summons a fire engine; the next morning we mark the burnt bedding piled up by the rubbish bags. Your boyfriend saw a man killed, running out across a side-road, no time for anything but. There'll be no more jaywalking, until next week, or the one after, when I will have forgotten. I want to learn what it means to be in love with London. Atop the bus and sweltering, I see a man help a woman, about to faint, into a car. On Oxford Street the oversized letters above each shop are covered in metal pins. In case what? Sparrows, nesting over Topshop. Pranksters with a will to climb, to be the very highest. On Westminster Bridge, reluctantly I am impressed by the dazzle, each pane glinting and the river wider than I knew. Before I leave we sit, drawn to the cool of St Giles-without-Cripplegate, enclosed by the Barbican's dream fulfilled: as the architect must have meant it, you say; people sunning on concrete, feet dangling over green pools, fountain-flecked. Milton was buried here, and Oliver Cromwell wed. Burned and built, the story of London. There is your old smile, and a new one too. A joke falls flat. Our days together are dwindling, I am losing you to these streets. On the train the country slips past, gold and grey. This is how it will be. We must be getting old.

Seven Breaths

Pam Plumb

Seven breaths. I wait for another, holding my own until chemistry demands I exhale.

I imagine you are pretending. Hiding in a corner of your own body, ready to jump out when I turn to leave. Perhaps you're skulking behind your double-sized liver, your face distorted by those feculent metastatic lesions. Or are you hoping I can't see you because your eyes are closed? That silly game we used to play when I was still your only grandchild.

I lean forward and peer at your eyelids. Should have saved your money on those creams. A crease-free stillness shrouds your eyeballs. Death does wonders for the skin. Its opacity is shocking. Almost verglas, the tissue holds black blue capillaries in suspension. The blood paused mid-journey. The ultimate in homeostasis.

Your hand in mine is still warm. I squeeze it once or twice. Morse code for my love. I know I won't find you sitting in the back room watching some shite telly programme or in the garden admiring your handiwork. Your ashes (you did say cremation, didn't you?) won't be any good for long discussions about your neighbour's cat or the dishing out of advice about which is the best margarine for lowering cholesterol. I forgot to ask you the meanings of all those sayings you bandy about. I should have made a list.

I wonder where you are. Has someone (Granddad?) come to greet you like in the movies? All white gowns and soft music through some back-lit tunnel. A snicker hijacks my grief as I hear you ooh-ing and aah-ing at the sight of him and I slap my hand over my mouth to keep in the giggles. I feel the nurses watching. More gulps of laughter tug at my chest and I heave in an effort to transform into a perfection of grief. Tears of unknown origin start to run and I can hold no more. Staggering from the room, a nurse tugs at my arm and I turn away knowing I will be unable to hide the hilarity from my eyes.

You always made me laugh in the wrong places.

Launch Pad

Diane Simmons

Our teacher sounds bored by the time she gets to me. 'So, Linda, what do you want to be when you grow up?'

I know I can't give the answer I want to, so I mumble, 'Nurse.' I'm the fifth girl to say that, so no one laughs, or throws their rubbers at me like they do when Rory McLean announces he wants to be an astronaut. The moon landing was on the TV last week and he's not shut up about it since.

'We dinnae have rockets in Scotland, stupit!' Shona Tarvet sneers at him when he gives his answer. 'We're no' American!'

Mrs Kelly tells Shona to be quiet, but I can tell she agrees with her.

I'm with Rory McLean on the astronaut thing. Not that I want to go into space, but I like to dream about things too. Like how I might one day get the chance to be a boy, or have blonde hair or be top of the class. I'd take top of the class over anything else though. Shona Tarvet and Rory McLean seem to take it in turns to come first in our class's tests. Every week when I watch one of them go up to the teacher's desk to choose a sweetie as a prize for being clever, I wish it were me. I'd choose a packet of Refreshers. They last ages if you suck them.

It's not the sweeties though, that I'm really after. I'd just like to be clever. I want to be able to do whatever I want when I'm grown up, not be stuck doing something boring. My mum has no patience with me. 'There's nothing wrong with being ordinary,' she says. 'Being clever's not the be all.'

I'd like the chance to find out.

The teacher's all smiles when it's Shona's turn. 'And how about you?' she asks.

'I'm no' sure.' Shona gives one of her sickly smiles. 'I like babies.'

Mrs Kelly smiles. 'Working with children can certainly be rewarding. Perhaps you should be thinking about becoming a children's doctor or a surgeon.'

Shona shrugs. 'I'm no' fussed about a job. I'd like to stay home like ma mum.'

Mrs Kelly looks like she's been slapped. She clears her throat and starts tidying the jotters on her desk like she always does when she's annoyed.

I wish I could be brave like Shona and Rory. They aren't bothered what people think. If I'd been them, I'd have had the guts to tell the teacher I want to be a doctor. It's not that impossible – my dad says that children develop at different stages. I've got long multiplication sorted now and last week I didn't have a clue.

When the teacher's busy quizzing everyone else, I sneak a peek at Rory McLean. He's drawing a rocket, pressing hard down on his jotter when he adds the clouds of smoke.

It's preparing to launch. Just like me and Rory.

Half-Life

Michael Marshall Smith

'You're sure about this?' the old man asked.

Sourdine nodded curtly. He'd told the man five times already, and explained his reasons. He'd signed a waiver and confirmed his intentions in writing, providing copious evidence that he was of sound mind. He was done talking.

'I have an opinion, if you're interested.'

Sourdine shook his head. The old man shrugged, and turned to the laptop on a stand positioned by the operating chair, where he consulted an array of images — a multi-perspective evocation of the patient's brain. He spoke softly as he made the final preparations, the bedside manner of the doctor he must presumably once have been.

'How will you go from here? Afterward?'

'There's a car waiting to take me home,' Sourdine said. 'All you have to do is call the driver and tell him I'm ready.'

'I meant after that.'

'I'm a wealthy man. I have made arrangements for my care. Now, please, let's get this done.'

Sourdine had been single for most of his life, pouring all his energy into business. Then he fell deeply in love with a woman who was already married. Her husband found out, the affair ended, she remained married.

Leaving Sourdine alone, in agony, broken. Unable to let go of what had happened, clinging to its echoes. Miserably watching it recede and dim, until he realized how he might halt the process.

Experience is the enemy.

It piles up, constantly. You touch things, smell them, taste them, see them. People talk to you. Your feet hurt. The odour of cooking bacon floats across your mind. Each of these sensations, these tiny beats of the perceived life, smothers the past, coating it with a sticky residue of the new, wretched evidence of time's passing — transparent coats of lacquer that inexorably cloud, obscuring your view of what you want to remember. The lost, eroding glory. Your mind is powerless against this. It leaps to what just happened, grabbing it. It loses sight of what came before, even if that once felt like the most glittering thing in your life.

After suffering three months of this Sourdine was taking steps to prevent it getting worse.

The old man conducted the procedure, using probes to deliver a series of electrical impulses to specific areas of the brain, leaving Sourdine without hearing, touch, taste, sight or the ability to smell.

Then he called the driver.

'If you'd have let me,' the old man told Sourdine, as they waited, 'I would have told you this. It will fade regardless. You'll feel it diminish, day by day. Feel yourself forgotten. You'll mine out your memories until they become memories of memories, then even less than that. You'll chase them like falling leaves around a dark, empty valley, and the ones you catch will crumple in your hands. Eventually there will be nothing left except you and emptiness. She'll still be gone. And there were so many other people out here to love.'

But, of course, Sourdine couldn't hear him.

Random

Calum Kerr

My shoulder's jostled in the precinct and she's gone: running, fleeing, flying.

"Oi!"

Her phone hits my shoe, her voice calls, "Sorrreeeee," and she's gone: a thought, a dream, a ghost, with arms swimming through the air, trainers drumming on the concrete, dark hair pulled back in the wind.

I bend and snatch and run after her, battering at the pavement with my coat streaming behind me.

"Superman!"

I see her dodge and weave, tying pedestrians in knots, and I follow, chasing and closing, her back pulling me on. The thrill of the race causes heads to turn, men and women watching us, wondering who is the victim, who is the aggressor; presuming to know the story we're writing with our beating feet.

A child points.

I'm laughing.

Red lights go green and she stops at the precipice of the road, gasping and grinning, bending to clutch her knees, ready to start again. Startled by my arrival, she stands but smiles.

"Your phone... You dropped it." I hold it out: an offering and a greeting.

She takes it from my hand, her fingers against mine, her eyes on mine, our breath beating out in time.

"Thanks."

"Why'd you run? No-one's chasing."

She says nothing. The lights change. She takes my hand and we launch ourselves across the road, running down the world.

Eating My Words
Marie Gethins

You said my name tasted sweet, like a sun-warmed peach in July. I loved watching you articulate the syllables, savouring your expression. Other words triggered different tastes inside your mouth. I learned which to avoid in the delicate buffet of our conversation.

You waited after my lecture on alabastron Greek vases, invited me for a coffee. Early on I'd picked you out from the crowd. While others took notes or dozed, you seemed mesmerised. At the café you leaned across the table, pushed me to talk. I thought my research fascinated you, but words were what you craved.

Later as we lay spent in damp sheets, you revealed your synaesthesia, repeating my name in a whisper. You coaxed me to speak, asking for more details and terms. I told you about handle designs on loutrophoros vases. How they were used for immersion rituals, buried in tombs of the unmarried. You stared at the ceiling, listened and licked your lips.

Three months on you tired of Ancient Greece. Spending hours in the university library, I assembled new verbiage to tempt you. Kush, Ming, Caddoan. I missed deadlines, gave excuses to friends, yet you remained unsatisfied.

Last week I cut across campus. Through a window I saw you in a Botany lecture. The screen title in blue bold: Medieval Physic Gardens. Words and pictures flashed: elecampane, myrtle, vervain, yarrow. From the front row, you watched Delphine Laurent form the words. Mouth parted, eyes bright – the look I thought you reserved for me.

I found you in the café with Delphine this afternoon.

Two smiles over latté froth, a text book of plant illustrations open between the cups. You stuttered an excuse that I brushed away. Opening my bag, I pulled out a special list and enunciated each entry. Steadfast, loyal, faithful, relationship, commitment, promise. You grimaced, distaste rising in your mouth. I continued as moisture beads formed on your face, your skin growing pale. Each taste noted beside the word, I relished creating the combination: garlic, chilli, anise, gentian, chalk, soil. You had told me how each bad flavour lingered for days, created acid that scalded your throat.

Halfway through you dashed for the toilet, hand over your mouth. You knocked a chair, jarred the table. Latté splashes disfigured intricate petals and roots.

I rolled up my list. 'You'll need this.' I pressed the paper scroll into Delphine's palm and squeezed her shoulder.

Walking past the toilet, I shouted, 'LOVE.' I heard you heave.

What We Do In Our Sleep

Tino Prinzi

'And I've tried it with sips of water, pieces of bread, bits of cracker and blueberries, and it happens every time. Swallow, count to five, and there it is. It shouldn't be like this, should it?'

'Have you changed your diet recently?'

'No.'

'Do you eat a lot of processed or fried foods?'

'Some, not much. I get my five a day most days, maybe.'

'Okay. Have you got any water with you?'

'Yep.'

'How about any food?'

'Yeah lots of stuff. Shall I get it all out?'

'Just something small please; I'd like to listen to your stomach Mr Humphries.'

'I've got blueberries.'

'That'll do.'

'You do believe me, don't you?'

'I – Well, I need to listen for myself, so if you could pop up on the table and pull up your shirt please.'

'That's cold.'

'Sorry. Okay, now eat some blueberries.'

'Did you hear it?'

'I think so. Sounded like–'

'Hissing – gets worse with water.'

'Could you try some for me?'

'Sure.'

'That's pretty loud.'

'I know. Sometimes there's a pain too like its scraping along my side or something. I do live in a hard water area though.'

'Is it always like this?'

'No, it makes different noises with milk or tuna.'

'And have you got any with you?'

'Yeah. On the left side, zipped pocket.'

'Do you mind?'

'No, course not.'

'Okay Mr Humphries, let's try some tuna. Sorry, it's going to be cold again.'

'Are you listening carefully?'

'Yes. You can roll down your top now Mr Humphries.'

'Don't you want me to try some milk?'

'No, it's fine, I have a diagnosis.'

'I'm not dying am I?'

'No. What has happened to you is quite clear now—'

'It's not hypochondria or anything like that.'

'Excuse me?'

'I know you can all see my notes and stuff on there.'

'No, well yes, but you're right: it's not hypochondria this time.'

'Oh. Good.'

'It appears you have swallowed a kitten in your sleep, Mr Humphries.'

'I've – what?'

'It's more common than you think. Did you know that people swallow on average three kittens in their lifetime?'

'No?'

'Yes – that's why your stomach purrs when you eat tuna. Normally the stomach acid digests the kitten like a really tough steak, but in rare cases the stomach acid is too weak and it stays alive, feeding on the food and fluid you consume like a parasite.'

'This doesn't make sense. How'd I swallow a kitten? I can't even swallow paracetamol tablets whole.'

'You'd be amazed what we do in our sleep.'

'Shouldn't I get a scan or go to the hospital or something?'

'There's no need. I'll prescribe you some medication that

should help you digest it, or you can wait until it grows big enough to find its own way out, which won't be pleasant for either of you. It's your choice.'

Coming Clean

Davina Jones

It was the delicate scent of lily of the valley that gave Billy
away. Miss Popple leaned over him and noticed he smelt
unexpectedly clean, floral even, she was sure she recognised
the aroma. Normally Miss Popple was very sensitive to the
feelings of the children in her class, but she was so surprised
she carelessly blurted out:

'Billy Fisherton, is that lily of the valley I can smell?'

'What?' He looked shocked. 'Lily's valley?'

Miss Popple regained her composure, and crouched next
to him.

'I was just thinking how very gorgeous you smell today,
you remind me of my favourite flower. It's lovely,' she said
quietly.

'Thank you, Miss.' Billy looked at his desk.

The following day the same thing happened, and Miss
Popple was surprised to see his finger nails were almost
clean, and while his clothes were still unwashed Billy was
smelling even stronger of lily of the valley. At break-time
she was unsettled further by his unlikely questions.

'Miss? Is it real expensive Lily's valley?' he asked.

'Err, not especially, it's just not so common and I happen
to like it.'

'Miss, if you were given a pack with soap and talcum
powder, would it cost loads?'

'I'm quite sure whoever gave it to you meant it as a very
special present. You're a lucky boy, Billy.'

'Didn't think it was anything special, didn't...' He looked
horrified. 'I better go, Miss.'

Amid the bustle of children and parents at the end of the
day Miss Popple watched Billy striding out of the

playground alone. He usually walked himself home, but something about him niggled Miss Popple. Later, she found his sweatshirt in the classroom and made up her mind to drop it back to him. She knew he lived in an old portacabin in the woods behind the school.

Miss Popple climbed over the stile and walked through the tall pines. Not so far away she saw Billy sitting outside his head between his knees.

'Billy!' she shouted, suddenly nervous of her intrusion into his world.

'Miss! What're you doing here?' He had been crying.

'I've got your sweatshirt, I know you've only got the one, thought your mum...'

'My mum?' He looked alarmed.

'I thought she might want you to wear it in the morning?' Miss Popple stopped. 'Billy, what's the matter?'

'I didn't mean no harm, Miss, borrowing it like that, the Lily's Valley, just she said make sure you stay clean, and I found it under her bed. I didn't know it were special, I just needed the soap, but the talcum powder it were fun to use but I never should've. When she gets back I am goin' to be for it.'

'How long's she been gone Billy?'

'Only two days so far, she said stay clean and none of 'em'll know I've been away. You won't tell nobody will you Miss, about her goin' away - please?'

A Shanty for Sawdust and Cotton

Sarah Hilary

It's the smell of timber which draws Jake to the yard, that and the drumming in the soles of his feet when he passes the turning for the dry dock. They're building in the yard, working with hammers; the earth shakes in the same spot every time. He feels the breeze beating on sailcloth, the fast flicking of flags and, when the men are cutting wood, the froth and fizz of the saw.

After a week or so, Jake gets up the courage to enter the shipyard. He finds the big doors ajar, silence packed inside. It's lunchtime. The men are taking a break. Jake can smell pickles and cheese.

'Hello,' he offers, a question for anyone who might be around. He tests the gap in the doors, turning his body sideways to slip through. Slim as a cake slice, Jake, that's what his mother always says.

Dusty air crowds round him. Cautiously he feels his way to the heart of the yard where the timber scent is strongest. Here, bowed and arched, is the carcass of a new ship. He follows it with his fingers, smoothing the flats of both hands over the ribcage of wood, laying his lips to the climbing curve of the stern. The timber is unpainted, raw and warm beneath his cheek.

Ships have been built in this yard for decades, Jake's teachers have explained, many sailing to the West Indies for sugar and spices, cotton and rum. The ships brought slaves too, ill treated, kept in the dark below deck. Jake moves to a spot midway between prow and stern where he crouches, pulling in his head to look like the pictures his teachers painted of the slaves crammed one on top of another in the hold.

Jake swallows the boiled sweet he's been sucking as he straightens himself out.

He climbs the ladder of the ship's ribs until he reaches the highest point of the prow, where he balances with both hands clasped behind him around the square joist at his back. He opens his eyes wide and sticks out his chin, straining his shoulders forward as far as he can without falling, imagining the roll and thunder of the sea around him.

Wally sees the boy enter the yard. It's midday. He's eating a sandwich and he figures if Jake wants to poke about it's no skin off his nose. The boy's been hanging around for weeks, but this is the first time he's come inside. Wally doesn't want to scare him away. He looks like a nice kid, always sucking sweets, more alert than most his age, even the ones who can see and hear.

'That's Jake Campbell. Blind and deaf, but he gets along OK. Sharp as a tack.'

Wally approves of the way Jake behaves around the yard, respectful, taking care near the dry dock. He's got a sailor's feel for the sea, Wally sees that straightaway, from the roll in the boy's walk and the way he comes upright when he gets too near the edge. He has a sailor's eyes too, burnt-blue by the sun.

Wally licks pickle from his chin, balancing the sandwich on the back of his hand. His fingers, twisted with arthritis, make a shelf ridged with knuckles where the crumbs collect.

The kid's climbing the ship. You'd never know he was blind, to watch him.

Wally's worked the yards all his life. He's a plain man. Wood's what he knows, not much more than that. He can tell oak from pine in a knock. Because of the arthritis he'll be finished soon but he can't complain, it's been a fair run. The only thing he wishes is that he'd been to sea in one of the ships he built. Too late for that now, with his hands the way they are, but Wally's not one for regret.

What's the kid up to? Dangerous-looking sport, but Wally keeps his own counsel. He doesn't want to startle Jake, for one thing.

'Look at him,' he thinks, seeing the smooth jut of the boy's chin, the slim span of his shoulders, strong fingers fastened behind his back. It's like he's growing out of the wood, a living part of the ship. Wally can smell the cotton-candy clean of him. He could teach Jake to handle a boat, just a small one. With those strong fingers and Wally's eyes—

They could set to sea, the blind deaf boy and the old man whose hands are curling into claws, sail the sun together to the edge of the world.

A Visitor From The Past

David Coss

Charles crosses the room to the CD player and brushes against the blouse which is flung over the back of a dining chair like a melting Dali clock. It has hung there ever since Mary died.

He selects Roy Orbison, nudges the edge of the disc into the slot and watches the machine suck in the rest of it. A gentle prod on 'play' and he crosses to the settee where he eases his creaking body onto the comfortable cushions ready to wallow in the requested strains, as if in the ecstasy of a hot bath on a bitter, winter's day.

He sees the blouse flutter in a current of chilling air, and looks round the room; the windows are closed, as is the door. He smiles, remembering the not too distant times - a place where he once believed in fairy princesses and shining knights.

'Knew you'd come. Happy birthday, Sweetheart. Always been a special day for you, hasn't it? ... Listen, it's our song.' He sings along. 'In dreams I walk with you. ... Now that brings back a few memories, Mary, doesn't it ?'

The blouse slides from the chair onto the carpet and, to Charles' eyes, becomes a silken mound which slowly starts to stir - the peak rises a fraction and then falls back again. These almost imperceptible movements continue, as did her ribcage those many times, during the last few months of her illness, where he would rest his head to assure himself with the reality that she was still breathing.

Chanel No. 5 tingles in his nostrils. It is stronger than he remembers, but it's still sweet, still gentle - still his Mary. It's been many months since he'd last known the bliss of inhaling it directly off her warm skin.

'Guess what I had for breakfast?' he asks. '... Damn it, knew you'd know. ... And, I had soldiers too. ... Jealous, hey? ... Do you remember those wonderful times we spent in Llandudno? ... Was thinking of going there for a day out last month. ... Couldn't.'

In Dreams ends and Only the Lonely encroaches into the room. The blouse freezes. Charles' nose ceases to recognise Mary. His smile drains away.

He crosses the room and picks up the blouse. Its softness is smooth and cool on the tips on his fingers, as was her cheek that last time he'd touched it.

Charles slumps back into his well-worn corner of the couch and reflects on the previous few minutes - the flames of the past, having been extinguished, now leave him in the chill of the present.

'If a handful of months was an eternity,' he thinks, 'how do I cope with the next twelve?'

A Sense Of Balance

Andy Jenkinson

A quick calculation: Assuming this roof is directly above the 5th storey, it must be about 75 or so feet up. Call it 25 metres. Metric for the win. Potential energy = m x g x h. So ≈ 250 times my mass. A lady never discusses her weight, so we won't explore that figure exactly thankyouverymuch. If I completely converted that into kinetic energy ($\frac{1}{2}mv^2$) I could rearrange it and cancel that embarrassing m, thus preserving my modesty. So v = the square root of 500. About 22 m/s. Jesus. What's that in miles per hour? I've got a conversion app that would trivialise that sum, but I daren't take my phone from my pocket. My arms are currently outstretched and aiding with my balance. All things considered, that's more urgent at this moment in time.

This would've been easy if I'd kept up gymnastics after highschool. The maths nerd who was also pretty good on the beam. That'd been my thing. Admittedly that was some time ago – my age had since trebled, and my m had nearly doubled. It's just like riding a bike, I hoped, albeit with rather more at stake if you fall off. Just concentrate on the basics: Look where I'm heading – at the end of the handrail, not at my feet – and only make small adjustments, not big movements. It was harder than I remembered it being, but back then I wasn't being distracted by the breathtaking view of the city's evening skyline, the gusting wind, or mental calculations of how fast I might be travelling when I hit the floor. Also the audience, such as they were, tended to be mainly supportive parents rather than jeering co-workers very vocally expressing how they wanted me to slip and plummet to my demise.

***

A quick calculation: I'd studied Farouk's form, and he wasn't likely to make it. He's over 30 (about 80% succeed), wears glasses (48%) and he hadn't visited the company gym in his probationary month (45%). The big one was his previous employment – only 29% of those who'd come from another job in the city managed to 'balance the books', as I'd learnt the initiation was called. If Farouk somehow managed *not* to fall, it'd really hurt me - I'd given 3/1 on him completing, and there had been lots of takers.

*

Unlike some of my co-workers I didn't actually cheer. I just drew a sigh of relief. Now would come the hard part – the inevitable press interviews whilst trying not to be distracted by the beautiful view from my office window, the glorious weather and my mental calculations of how much I'd just won. Concentrate on the basics: "The thoughts of the company are with Farouk's family. Some people are tragically unable to cope with the pressures of a job in the city. Perhaps he just couldn't find a work/life balance. What a senseless loss."

Hosting
Christopher Allsop

The salesman won't leave. But how had he come in? Somehow he had moved from door, exterior of, to sofa, interior of.

It is said that self-preservation is our strongest instinct. For me, it is hosting. I carry over a slice of my homemade salted caramel paired with a cup of my afternoon brew; a blend of chamomile, lavender, linden flower and a dose of valerian—dense and aromatic. In the afternoons, I sit where the salesman is sitting and inhale it, dissolve into it.

The salesman has a briefcase, blue and deep. My husband had a briefcase, black and slim, with locks of brass (code: 007; my idea). A present to mark his promotion. I polished the brass for his trip as I would polish his shoes, to a ruddy shine. He was a fool around alcohol, but a quiet, amusing man with a gift for remembering things that hadn't seemed memorable. When he left, framed in the door with his bespoke suit and luminous shoes, I can't tell you what effect it had. It was sexual. I kissed him; he pulled away, surprised. He left his shoes on the riverbank, caked in red mud. At first, I protested that they weren't his shoes (the mud had coloured them oxblood). Bearing his belongings home, I noticed that the mud had spilled over the top of the left shoe and stained the patterned interior. Did he notice the mud's cold touch? Or is this how this is done: with your notice switched off? But how is *that* done?

The salesman is watching me. He has finished his caramel, and the afternoon brew is untouched, cold and dull, its scent withdrawn from the air. I roll my wedding ring around my finger. How long have I been with this man? Salesmen like this are often on commission only. How can you waste the time of a salesman when his time is so precious? How can you let him know that you have wasted his time when his time is so precious? One brings agony to me, the other agony to him. I am filled up.

I say: "I've changed my mind, thank you."

He does not leave. It makes no sense. But now the kettle is whistling and I have served him a fresh tea—Assam, his choice—and he settles around to face the garden. Perhaps if I explain myself, I can excuse myself. Explain how, around this time, I like to sit in the lounger that I have dragged out beyond the garden. Wrapped in a blanket, I look across the desert, towards the mountains. At first, I did this because I could not bear to remain inside without anyone coming through the door.

But one cannot abandon one's guests. He agrees to stay for dinner. The palms are carving up the sunset. In the pan, the oil fizzes and pops. From beneath the smell of the meat rises the chemical hint of underarm.

His hands take my waist.

I Am No Good at Video Games
Nik Perring

My girlfriend is trying to give me up and I am no good at video games. I never have been.

When my girlfriend gave up smoking cigarettes she started eating apples instead. One to replace each cigarette. When that didn't work I said, 'Hey, honey, I'd like to give them up too. Let's do this together.'

I inherited the apples and she moved on to biscuits – one digestive to replace each cigarette. She got big for a time but it worked. I just ended up with hating apples and with different bowel movements. We both got back to normal after a little while. In the end, we both won.

Once we got ourselves smoke-free my girlfriend decided she wanted to give up coffee. It was making her hyper, she said. It was making her hands shake. That was about the time she stopped wearing nail polish. This time she chose to have a glass of juice to replace coffee – one glass to replace each mug – but, like the apples, that didn't work out so well either. She got annoyed with all the trips to the bathroom. So I helped her, said, 'If you can give up coffee, honey, I'll lay off the booze.' So I ended up on juice in the evenings while she moved on to grapes. I'd find pips everywhere – on the kitchen top, on the coffee table, on the arm of the sofa, on our dressing table, on the bathroom windowsill. She left a trail in stones.

Now she's trying to give me up. She hasn't said it in so many words, but I know her. I know how she thinks. I've noticed how every time I go to touch her, to kiss her, even start a conversation she'll move away from me and go into the kitchen.

I think she's replacing me with oranges. One for every kiss.

So I've given up TV. I borrowed a games console from my

59

friend. I've taken up playing video games.

While my girlfriend gorges on oranges – she must be on twenty a day now – I fire up the machine and start shooting things. While she's filling the flat with orange peel and while the air inside it is thick and cutting and citrusy, I sit in front of the TV, the controller in my hand, my fingers and thumbs tapping and strumming plastic and rubber, hard. But I'm no good. I keep dying. Over and over, I die.

But that's fine. I'm okay with it. It's either that or oranges.

Old Friend Dinner

Amy Mackelden

I want to know how your skin tastes and don't say, "Lick it." This just isn't enough. On TV, cannibal's akin to vegetarian diet, only as awkward as gluten-free or lactose-intolerant, no absolute judgement, as I am these things and I still want to slice your skin thin like crispy strips in California rolls and take much more than I should in my mouth at once for risk of seaweed splitting, which sounds sexual but isn't, honestly. It's very rarely sex when I think of you. Although, rare is not never, is it?

After your skin, I'm going to select an organ according to an internet recommendation. Cookbooks didn't catch up yet. Demand for print's 18 months off, so blogs are best bets and I'll comment on how well it went; a LIKE is worth more than eye contact. And my finest blades will understand lung intricacy the way Brad Pitt knows career longevity and, like chicken breasts on my thumb pads, I'll feel your body give under what pressure I have.

You may think together, unchopped, is better. To have your weight on top of me, rib cage complete and heart beat tick like crickets or a kettle click off. But this is not true, if episodes are believed like Bible supported testimonies, as Lindsay Lohan's reality show is, or it isn't? I wish it were simple, a high school date where you just ask and, once out of ten, the person says yes. Except, based on Facebook text, when you said, "Let's never get in a confined space like ever," I knew that you'd come at behest. I get a sense. So when are you free next?

The Well

A. Joseph Black

It's now my third or fourth hour in the well, and I'm resigned to my fate. It isn't unpleasant down here: cool, dark. Everything seems extraordinarily vivid, as if I'm seeing it through air which is clearer, more transparent, than the air up above: the glossy black wet stones and the opulent green moss, clumped in plump sumptuous cushions around the circular wall. I'm not hurt, not badly, I don't think. I just need someone to find me.

I've been watching a caterpillar on the floor of the well. It's the most extraordinarily virulent green colour. And fat. As long and as fat as my thumb. It undulates along a large pale leaf by my foot until it reaches the edge, where it begins to nibble. Then it ripples back across the same leaf and nibbles from the other side. Although there is no reason to this, it does it repeatedly: ripple and nibble, side to side, ripple and nibble. It becomes rather beguiling, hypnotic. Even if I could move my head (I can't) I'm not sure I could tear my eyes away from it.

My reverie is broken by a muted shrieking and odd skittering sound. A twig lands on my head, and at my feet a starling appears. Its pink legs and yellow beak jar my eyes amid the dark, muted green-brown palette of the well. I can see that the bird's injured: one wing is damaged, possibly broken. It struggles to its feet and inexpertly begins to move around. I wonder if there's anything I should - or could - do. Then the starling sees the caterpillar. Its beak darts forward, almost quicker than the eye, and with a fierce flash of green the caterpillar has gone.

5D

Ed Broom

The Empire was dying. Peeling paintwork, the odd leak and talk of asbestos were bad enough. A shiny new Cineworld on the edge of town proved terminal.

All the cool kids (and me and Will) had to be there for the last picture show. They were going out in style with a midnight screening of the original Texas Chainsaw Massacre to be presented, said the poster, "In Fabulous 5D: Dread, Decay, Depravity, Desperation and Death!"

Will took his favourite seat right at the end. Usually we had the whole row to ourselves. For maybe the first time since Titanic, the place was packed. House lights down, no trailers – no point – BBFC certificate and the narrator began: "The film which you are about to see..."

When the hitchhiker pulled out his knife, some goon ran down the aisle slashing at the already slashed seats. That got some screams. One or two of the girls tried to leave.

When the kids saw the meat on the hooks, we felt small fleshy lumps land on our heads and laps. Nothing scary about that until you breathed in. Next to me, the bearded bloke gagged.

When Kirk, the first victim, was about to enter the house, some other guy jumped out with something in his hand - a mallet? - and pretended to hit a random member of the audience in the head. They must have used fake blood. People nearby ran for the exit.

When Leatherface cranked up his chainsaw, mallet guy reappeared with his very own power tool. He strode into the crowd revving ever higher. That's when we all freaked out.

People running and falling and yelling and slipping. A

maniac on the loose. That stench of bad meat. It was awesome.

I escaped with a few bruises. Will wasn't so lucky. Nowadays I drive us out to Cineworld. I push him into the disabled area, then sit nearby. I always did prefer an aisle seat.

Please Remain Silent for the Benefit of Other Library Users (In Hushed Tones)

Debbie Young

Why, Miss Blossom, how lovely to see you back in the Reading Room, it's been a while, has it not? I hope you've been keeping well. The Times? Yes, I've finished with The Times. Please be my guest. No, no, I've definitely finished.

I was just going to toddle along to the Science section until I saw you. Yes, Neuroscience, actually, it's a new interest of mine. I've been spending a lot of time in that department lately. Fascinating stuff, absolutely fascinating.

Just yesterday I came across a fact I'd never known before. Tell me, have you ever noticed that although the smell of polish hits you the minute you enter the library, you cease to notice it after a while? Apparently, that's nature's way. We're all programmed to stop noticing a smell, good or bad, within moments of first sensing it.

Yes, unpleasant smells too. Yes, I suppose it is a blessing. That must be why that air freshener company has been advertising a device that alternates between two different perfume reservoirs – so that the user is constantly reminded that it's working.

No, no, I don't watch much commercial television either. I just happened to switch over by mistake.

But the same applies to all the other senses, according to the book I've been reading over in the Science section. If you hear a sound repeatedly, it fades into the background.

Yes, trains passing your flat at night, that's an excellent example. You only notice them when they stop – when there's a strike and they don't run. I've noticed that too. You're so right. Next time I'm kept awake by the silence of striking trains, I shall – there, I shall say it! – I shall think of you.

And have you noticed how the same food or drink, day after day, ceases to be pleasurable? Yes, that first cup of proper English tea after a trip abroad is always the best, you're quite right.

And as to touch, well, I never notice the cat curled up against my arm on the bed at night, once she and I have settled down. Your cat sleeps on your bed too? Sooty sleeps on your bed, curled up into the small of your back? Oh, Miss Blossom, I say! I wonder whether our cats would be friends if they met?

The other sense? The fifth one? Does it work for the sense of sight?

Well, do you know, I am at odds with the book on that one. Because, Miss Blossom, because – and I don't care if the librarian is looking daggers at me since you ask – no matter how often I spot you in this Reading Room, and no matter how long I gaze at you before you look up and notice me, I will never tire of the sight of you . Oh Miss Blossom, dare I ask? Would you care to join me for the afternoon in the Science Section?

The Law of Attraction in Action

Sonya Oldwin

Even before I look out the window I know the snow hasn't melted over night. Maybe I worded an order wrong somewhere along the way.

Some people – the ones who, I assume, care about me – tried to talk sense into me. I wouldn't listen. I was about to follow my dream, after all, and this sort of reaction is what you have to expect. The cautious, the nay-sayers, the weak who don't dare to go after their dreams – they want to keep you in your place. Because you make them look bad if you go and find yourself. You have to ignore them – common knowledge for the avid practitioner of personal development.

Undeterred, I packed my things and went up into the mountains. To freedom. I believed in myself. I believed that if I wanted it enough, sent the right messages to the Universe, I'd attract the right sort of life.

It worked okay in the beginning. I went up in early summer and for almost a month, the weather was beautiful. I was in paradise.

It was a fluke, of course. The first thunder storm I experienced gave me a glimpse of what the Universe had in store for me. A tree collapsed after a lightning strike. It buried my well underneath. If it hadn't been for the three days of deluge, I'd not have had any water. I managed to repair the damage somewhat, but getting water out became hard work. It's just as well there was nobody to complain about my sketchy personal hygiene.

Autumn came, and with it the gales. I spent several days cooped up in my little hut, too scared to venture outside. Which was a good thing, given the amount of branches that were shaken loose off the trees. On the bright side, I thought, if I collect all the wood, I'll be fine for firewood until I need to leave for the winter.

I told everyone I'd be down before the winter. Only the snow came a lot earlier than I expected. I didn't know how to read the signs until it was too late. I went to bed on a late autumn night and woke up to a winter morning.

I've no hope of getting away. I'm cut off from civilisation, there's not much food left. It's what I wanted. The cut-off part, that is, not the starvation.

I came here to find out what life is all about once you've stripped away all the layers of sense and meaning mankind has added over the centuries.

Turns out it's about dying.

The Water Is Clear

Emmaleene Leahy

Scales fall away. Peeling sunburnt skin is tight like last years t-shirt. I feel relief as I dive in, the splitting cracking sensation gone.

The water is clear in a fake blue mosaic way. Nothing lives here. It reeks of bleachy chemicals. The sun still pours its heat on me.

Hairs prickle to alertness as a shadow creeps and crawls, growing over me, blocking out the sun. That's how I know he's behind me sneaking up but I don't flinch.

His hand cups the crown of my head, shoves me down. I resist, stretch my head towards the sky then submit. I allow his force submerge me under the water once I've filled my lungs. Bubbles of air tickle my lips as I release them, chlorine stings my nostrils.

"Minnow" he taunts.

I splash and struggle then stop. I let go of all effort, go totally limp, allow myself to float up, motionless. I play his game or rather he plays mine. At ten years of age I am only up to his nineteen year old shoulder but in the water I am superior.

I drink in the flash of panic on my big brother's distorted face as I peer up at him from under the undulating ripples.

I've spent the summer, sunrise to sundown, flitting and drifting in the river. I'd dart and glide to sink down into the silent depths to probe and explore the secrets enclosed like marrow in bone in the smooth stones on the riverbed. I'd weave between ragged weed to find the treasures dragged under the froth, swept up in the current then heaved and hauled by the water's flow to the mortuary below.

He's been in the shade of the library studying for

university exams or off with his girlfriend. He booked this holiday as a romantic reward for all his hard work before Mama's diagnosis.

Water spills over the edges as I explode out of the water. I wallow in the look of relief on my big brother's face and swallow it down. With his expression inside me, at my core, I will always feel safe with him to protect me. I know that he won't ever let anything happen.

When Mama passed, he decided to take me on this holiday. I'm not sure what happened to his girlfriend or if she even existed in the first place. Maybe she was just a story he made up to stop Mama worrying. Maybe he was going to bring Mama with him as a surprise to celebrate passing his exams to thank her for all her hard work bringing us up alone, for doing such a great job. Maybe he dumped his girlfriend so he could be free to look after me. I don't really know.

All I know is that it's just me and him now safe in our sense of belonging to each other.

Eye of the Beholder

Miranda Roszkowski

He had a cut on his forehead, probably from the brambles outside his house. Examining it in the bathroom mirror, Nathan could see it was red, swollen and starting to weep.

He found a plaster in a dog-eared carton at the back of the cabinet and covered the sore. Quite possibly a result of drunken 'high spirits', it wasn't something you wanted people to ask about.

Not wanting to miss his appointment, Nathan jogged downstairs, skipping the last step and landing with a flourish.

He prepared his cereal, black coffee and vitamin pill efficiently. He wasn't normally a vitamin guy, but at 32, perhaps it was time to live a little healthier. The two grand he was getting for the clinical research wasn't bad either.

He left his dirty bowl in the sink with the others, downed the last of his coffee and grabbed his coat. As he opened the door the November wind made his eyes water. His forehead felt wet too. The cut, or whatever it was, had started to weep again. He wiped his eyes, pulled a hat from his pocket and set out.

At the clinic he was met by a medic who introduced himself as Doctor Collins. Tall with a sharp nose and dark brown eyes, Nathan couldn't pin-point his accent, which made him sound like he was reading from an auto-cue.

"Nathan! You're on the Miratron trial! How are you feeling?"

"Good actually" Nathan smiled, dimples on show. "Really good."

"Helping you see things differently?"

"Yeah, I think so."

The doctor beamed as he prepared his tools for the usual tests. They chatted throughout the check-up and Nathan decided he liked Doctor Collins, though he was a little eccentric.

As Nathan scrawled his autograph over the box to confirm he was happy to continue the trial, Collins pointed to the plaster on Nathan's head.

"Do you mind if I take a look?"

"Go for it, mate."

Nathan was grateful for the advice. His forehead was starting to sting and he would probably have to get a professional to look at it. The less time spent in foul-smelling GP's waiting rooms the better.

"Could you just close your eyes?"

Nathan felt his shoulders tense slightly, but as the doctor leant over he did what he was told.

Doctor Collins peeled off the plaster and Nathan recoiled. It seemed like a bright light was shining straight into his brain.

"Don't worry," he heard the doctor say. The light was less bright now. Nathan blinked and suddenly things were clearer, he could make out Doctor Collins above him, smiling his strange smile.

But, Nathan realised with horror, his eyes were still closed.

The doctor chuckled and handed him a small mirror. "What did I tell you? Miratron helps you see things in a whole new way!"

Nathan's hands shook as he took in his reflection. In the middle of the raw, pussing swelling on his forehead was a third eye, blinking.

Angus Hears Things

Jane Roberts

Angus isn't like other children, and today is far worse than
most other days. His parents and teachers all know how
sensitive he is. It's been explained to his classmates and
family – and family friends – just how sensitive he is. When
his grandmother dropped her knitting needles on the stone
kitchen floor at Christmas, Angus heard a million icicles in
the Arctic drop and shatter – and shatter – and shatter...
The echoes still haunt him when he sleeps. If he sleeps.
Even the window cleaner scraping sugar lumps from the
sugar bowl and plopping them into his cup of tea had no
idea that in Angus' soundscape it was the collapse of a
jagged mineshaft and tidal wave of an angry ocean.

So today Angus walks down the street, keeping to the
regimented metal railings and inanimate brick walls, careful
to avoid the confusions and confrontations of sound – not
just the child-swallowing cracks in the pavement. His
parents know it's one of those days. Some sympathetic
bystanders note the way Angus clutches at his ears and
shakes his head. But not those other pedestrians, who
march along, disregarding the cracks in the pavements – not
-yet-late for their meetings, but with eyes glued to
smartphones anyway.

The dogs notice though. It's hard for them not to take
offence. When someone avoids you like that, it's really hard
not to take offence. So they decide to ask him what it's all
about, in a casual way, you understand. But dogs are very
good at frightening children when they have to speak by
baring their hooked fangs – yellowed by meat juices over
the years.

A Pug waddles up to Angus, who already can hear

Mount Etna erupting on its rasping breath.

"Little boy, what's your name?" asks the polite Pug.

Angus now knows just how bad a day it really is. This has never happened before. As he runs to the sanctuary of the family car, a Chihuahua sidles up to the dejected Pug.

"It's Angus, his name is Angus", says the Chihuahua. "Don't worry, it's not your fault. Only some humans can hear us."

"Ah, that explains a lot". The Pug gazes after Angus – wide-eyed and stoic.

*

Angus doesn't come down for breakfast the next day. His mother goes up to his bedroom. She sits on his bed. Strokes his hot head. Takes his temperature.

"What's wrong, Angus?"

He looks at his mother – hesitates – then decides he can ask the question that has bothered him so.

"Mummy, can dogs talk? I mean, like humans can talk."

She ruffles his hair. "Don't be silly, Angus!"

Yes, he thinks, I'm being silly. And he almost believes that until the Border Collie from No.7 shouts through his open bedroom window:

"Angus, you know she's wrong."

The Visitors From Out of Town

Tim Stevenson

The first time, at the end of the hot summer when the roads had melted and our dogs slept on the cool stone of our doorsteps, they only stayed for a day.

They stared up at the trees and smiled at the children who followed them around. They dipped their feet in the river and lay in the fields and picked their teeth with the long grass of the meadow.

Then they left and we all waved them off and watched until they were out of sight.

The second time it was during the big snow, their tiny footprints around the statue in the square led away towards the fields and the farm up on the hill.

The next day Tom Crawford shooed them out from amongst the cows in his barn and Maisie Jackson shouted down from her bedroom window that she could have sworn she'd heard one scratching around in her attic, but it might have been her missing cat.

The children still followed them but now they were the only ones who waved goodbye when it was time to go.

The third time was in the spring when the daffodils were pushing up into the sun and Maisie's funeral had dressed the village in somber clothes and filled the air with whispers.

They gathered on the green and faced each other, communing in their high-pitched voices and pointed at each building, each person who passed by, and made notes before they left their little metal suitcases piled on the grass and gathered in front of the butcher's window.

This time the children left them alone, they were no longer fascinated by our visitors' grey skin, their black-almond eyes and their little teeth, like sharks.

Friday Roses

Cath Bore

The red roses Brian sends every Friday are delivered to the house, bound in a tight bundle. The taut rubber band pinks my fingers and thorny stems long and tentacular splice my skin as I unpick the stubborn brown rubber. My fingers cut and bleed but they push the flowers into a vase.

'Have they arrived, the flowers?' Brian rings up and asks, as always.

'Yes, they've arrived. Thank you.'

'And do you like them?' He says this each time too.

'I love them.'

He makes me say it every week, forces me to lie. Sometimes I think I hate the roses more than I despise Brian. They offer up no scent, shiny plastic petals scratch the end of my nose as he forces me to sniff them and inhale plain air that smells of tap water.

Flowers every week, how romantic, everyone says. You're so lucky.

'Yes,' I smile. 'I'm lucky.'

My cracked ribs creak as I force uncomfortable words out from lips stiff and awkward with lies.

In the end, all it takes is a little push. I watch Brian fall down the stairs, arms in frantic circles, hands grabbing air, gob flapping silently. He breaks. I taste copper in my mouth and smell its perfume, realise I've bitten my tongue, held it between my teeth as I watched him windmill downwards. Relief washes through me like a flood but the police believe my tears.

The following Friday roses arrive as usual, red like blood.

Parched

Jeanette Sheppard

The emerald necklace swings from our sycamore tree. The sun catches the emeralds and mottles a clump of dried out leaves. How did she reach? I suppose she stood on the garden table. My insides jerk at the thought. She's safe now though, on the bench, her pale legs – *yes, they're still shapely, even at seventy two, Mum* – outstretched under her poppy skirt that she's hitched above the knee. She gazes up at the emerald glints; her hands in her lap, upturned as if about to catch something.

My instinct had been to shout: *What are you doing?* It's been a tough day. People don't like it when there's a drought and they have to collect their water in a bucket from a stand in the street. I watch her for a moment; she hasn't heard me. There's a new bald patch in her thin white hair, just behind her left ear with the soft brown birth mark.

I can't afford emeralds, of course, they were Gran's. *For a rainy day, Magda*, she said. *I've told your mother they are for your rainy day.*

I inch my way towards Mum across the gravel but the crunch alerts her. She turns her head and smiles her lop-sided smile. She clicks her dentures back into place. 'Where did you find the necklace, Mum?'

'A mother always discovers her little girl's secret hiding places.'

'I see.' She turns back to the glints in the tree. 'Why did you hang the necklace up there?'

'You are a silly girl. Everything's parched. We need rain don't we? Rain comes from high up doesn't it?'

I look up at the emerald drops. Above the sycamore the sky is clear blue. Not a cloud in sight and at the same time a breeze cools my face.

Masha's Burning Memory
Selina SIAK Chin Yoke

When the men came with their burlap sacks, Masha was crouching in the attic with slices of the duck meat her mother Yalena Ivanovna had set aside for smoking. Downstairs, their huge oven was lit, and smoke poured out of a chute into their farmhouse. The gruff voice at the front door could only be their neighbour's, his hostility evident even from the roof.

'Yalena Ivanovna,' he bellowed, 'we have orders to search your house and land.'

'Sergei Oleksandrovich, good day. Pray, what are you looking for?'

This question brought only the sound of trampling boots. Masha tip-toed to a corner, knowing not to make a squeak; from a tiny crack she spied at least six men. In the middle was Sergei, surveying their bread and cabbages with a sneer. His twisted mouth made Masha start. She had always been afraid of him, even on his first visit, when he was still a lowly Party member; now that he had risen in rank and fervour, she felt quite sick. Masha crushed her nose against the straw-strewn floor to gain a better view.

Yalena Ivanovna stood glowering, a hand on each hip. Masha prayed silently; now was not the time for pride.

'We are here for the rest of your goods.'

'You know I have already given everything. We had an agreement, don't you remember?'

'Then was then, now is now.'

'But I have no more to give. I have five children.'

'No more to give? What do you call this?' Sergei gestured towards the table. 'And the wheat in your fields? You keep chickens too, don't you? Horses, cows? Nothing to give! Bah!'

'You cannot take my chickens, horses, cows or wheat.' From her mother's steely posture, Masha could sense trouble brewing.

'Still behaving like a landowning farmer, are you? Once a kulak, always a kulak! We'll teach you!'

Masha heard a scuffle, and then scraping. The men snatched up whatever they could: bread and cabbages, jars of beans, pickled vegetables from the corner cupboard. They stuffed their burlap sacks. Sounds rang out in Masha's head: the table overturning; her mother shouting 'You will stop now!'; someone falling over; the brittle cracking of jars; the fury in Sergei's voice 'Now we really will teach you!'; her mother's hard panting; a cry of 'Hold her feet!'

Four men dragged Yalena Ivanovna, horizontally, each holding onto a limb.

When their oven door creaked, Masha did not know what to think. The walls trembled, but Masha could not believe. It was only when her mother screamed, wrenching her soul in such a way that it would never heal, that Masha understood. The whole of her came alive: every cell, every nerve, even senses she did not know she possessed. She shivered. Saliva rose in her throat. She cried. Masha wanted to die.

Through the billowing smoke, a figure rose on the makeshift ladder. Masha glared at Sergei with burning spite. Dust and ashes, she thought. You will be nothing but dust and ashes.

Tomorrow We Will Return, But It May Not Be Sunny

Cassandra Parkin

"How many we got?" Bill peered into the meat-wagon and sucked his teeth. "Just the two?"

"Things ain't what they used to be," said Mick.

"That's one for each of them," Stephen said. Noob cheerfulness.

"How they expect us to raise a decent size on this," said Bill.

"Ah, well." Mick sighed. "Gator's waitin'."

They dragged the meat-wagon down the canal path. Bill on the left pole, Mick on the right, Stephen on watch-out. (Useful rumour: an apparent cold one once lurched back to frantic life and escaped, howling, into the wilderness. No actual proof, but the unions treated it like gospel; so, three to a wagon, no exceptions.) The meat, warmed by the sunshine, sent up a spiral of rot.

"Smashing day for it," said Stephen.

"Rain tomorrow," said Bill.

"Got to enjoy it while it lasts," Mick agreed.

"Can't do with too much," said Bill. "Gators need swamp. Here."

"But the feeding station," said Stephen. Mick smiled, remembering the time he was young enough to go by the book.

"There." Bill pointed to two bumps on the surface. "Waiting for us."

Stephen swallowed. Mick patted him on the back.

"Floatin' protein," he said heartily. "Another month, he'll be ready to harvest. Meantime, grub's up…"

Other crews made noobs assist with the chuck – some even insisted they swung the ankles, the part most prone to detachments. But Bill was a decent sort, and took the ankles himself. Mick grabbed under the armpits, counted "One – two – three -". They lifted, swung, released, saluted. Watched the meat disappear beneath the water. Tactfully ignored Stephen vomiting into the campions.

"We all come to it," said Bill at last; the signal to drop the salute.

"Yep," Mick agreed. "Cheer up, Stephen, you get used to it."

They picked up the poles and walked along the tow-path. Stephen gulped at his water-bottle, sacrificing a precious mouthful to rinse and spit.

"Got one for you," Mick said to Bill.

"'S'hear it."

"Bloke gets called up to HQ. Goes into the restaurant, gets sat down. Waiter comes, big silver dome. Lifts it, on the plate's a slice of chicken. The bloke eats it. Goes home, tells his wife, *I had chicken up at HQ. Go on*, she says. *What was it like?* And the bloke shrugs and says, *To be honest, just like alligator...*"

Bill and Mick chuckled, then fell silent. Stephen smiled frantically, hoping to see the joke. They passed the feeding station, peeled off their gloves and sat to eat their sandwiches. Stephen excused himself and slipped modestly behind a tree.

"Mick," said Bill.

"Boss?"

"He didn't get it. The chicken joke."

"Too young," said Mick.

"But we're the last ones, Mick," said Bill. "The last ones who'll remember how things used to be. When we're gone -"

"You okay, boss?" asked Mick, startled.

Bill hesitated, then shrugged.

"Sure." He stood up, took hold of the wagon-pole. "Best get going. Gator's waitin'."

Chekhov's Gun

Nigel McLoughlin

The protagonist in this story does not yet exist. But we believe they do and that is what is important. As someone opens their eyes, the world comes into being. They see the hair colour in the bathroom mirror. There is a carton of auburn hair dye on the mirror shelf. It has been recently used. Standing there in a rather crumpled business suit, the neck of which is open, they explore the contours of their body. The clothes hang well, but there is some tenderness at the throat and pain in the left-side scalp. A quick inspection shows traces of dried blood.

After some rummaging, business cards are produced from the suit pocket. People don't carry multiple copies of business cards not their own, so the name on the card attaches to the bearer. Now a name is known. This feels odd: like having to be reminded.

The dusty radio in the corner says this is Friday and extends a welcome to another day on Planet Earth using what feels like an instantly recognisable and sonorous voice. It also announces quite clearly that there has been no cleaning, at least not in the vicinity of the radio, in quite a while. There are no signs of life in the kitchen, no dishes, no cups, not a scrap to eat anywhere. Here, wherever here is, doesn't seem lived in.

There are no memories. Prior to waking up, it is almost as if nothing existed at all. It might even be that there have been a series of other selves, all waking up, all finding and reinventing the world anew. This world, which so far extends only to the bedroom, bathroom and kitchen of what is assumed to be a bedsit, makes itself in the slow movements to the window.

The street is almost quiet. Everyone looks to be somewhere else. A small and wiry dog is barking at something that cannot now be seen, or perhaps, the thought occurs, something missing and which should by rights be there. Maybe the dog is alert to the absence. What must be streets away, a sound intrudes into memory, and is experienced as an ice-cream van. There is uncertainty that it might not be, and it seems to be moving into the distance.

Something lies on the table in the kitchen pointing away. It is warm and heavy as it is hefted. There are traces of blood. Beside it, is a crumpled note in a hand that provokes no recognition, but also no surprise. It reads: 'I never used it'. The note is creased, and put in a pocket.

As though realizing what needs to happen next, they walk over to the door, pull down the handle and set it ajar as they go outside. There is no hand to reach back and pull it closed, no comforting click. The door swings. A gap closes to a paper-edge of light, and the whole world is a wiry dog that keeps barking, barking.

Spaghetti And Meat Balls
Colin Watts

DTI Peter 'Porky' Pearson scans his heavy-laden bookshelves. Stroking his belly with one hand and holding a half-eaten pork pie in the other, he's ruminating on the Mantini case. He wonders how 'one fat bastard' as his colleagues have dubbed said chef can have just disappeared off the face of the earth.

'Don't know about finding a needle in a haystack,' said Robinson; 'more like hiding a whale in a paddling pool.'

Porky is aware, not for the first time, that he would rather be reading about villains in the company of a tumbler of Jamesons and some decent cheese, than having to go out and catch them. But good food, whiskey and rare books do not come cheap. Porky has a well-honed nose for the pleasures of life, but also for the thoughts and deeds of low-life scum. He soldiers on.

He finishes the pork pie, licks his fingers and squeezes his love handles. Until recently, he's felt quite comfortable in his body, confident that his sleazy appearance – a couple of stone overweight, hair a tad long, suit creased, unfashionable and a size too small – belies an intellect of sharpened steel. He slips into his tartan lounge-wear, with its comfortably draw-strung trousers and goes to the kitchen for a top-up and a think.

It has been three weeks since Mario Mantini, head chef of The Fat Cat, a pretentious canal-side restaurant frequented by bankers and drug dealers, went missing. He was the last to leave on Saturday night and never returned. He lived alone, was never known to socialise, yet appeared to have no enemies. All the staff had decent alibis and all, Porky observed, were overweight, bar second chef Luciano

Alampi, who stood out like a strand of spaghetti in a plate of meat balls.

'Signor Mantini,' he'd said with a sniff and a tear, 'he was one-a fatta bastard, but he cooked up a storm and we loved him.'

Back before his bookshelves, Porky scans the titles. He knows he's looking for something, but is not yet quite sure what it is. His eye roams over *The Thin Man* by Dashiell Hammett, *Survival of the Fattest* by Stephen Cunnane, then lights on *The Unquiet Grave* by Cyril Connolly. He has a sudden flashback of Alampi sniffing his fingers while relating Mantini's culinary skills and gets a *déjà sent* of roasting meat. *"Inside every fat man there is a thin one trying to get out."* flashes into his mind. He sniffs his fingers, shudders, and has a vision of God holding Adam's spare rib and wondering what it might taste like, grilled with barbecue sauce. Alampi's statement and the Connolly quote rearrange themselves in his head. He bangs his forehead with his palm.

'Eureka! Thank you, Cyril!'

He rings the night team.

'Mike,' he says, 'pull in Alampi now. Get a shit sample off that skinny bastard and bring in any meat from his fridge and freezer. DNA results on my desk eight-thirty sharp.'

Sun Synchronous Satellites

Andy Lavender

"We're from Earth Observation," said the smiling woman waving a gold badge in front of Selena's eyes. "Remote Sensing Department. May we come in?"

Selena blocked the slice of the open door. "What's this about?"

"We'd prefer to talk inside." The woman took a step into the apartment, wedging herself between the door and its frame. Selena felt the woman's leather jacket pressing against her body, and her nose was flooded with hints of vanilla and star anise. She stepped back and the woman strode past. Selena held the door for her companion, but no -one followed.

Stood in the centre of the room, the woman wore a two piece leather suit the colour of a red morning sky. Her eyes were like shadows, over which she wore a pair of glasses with only one lens and her black hair was pulled back into a tight pony tail which forced her to smile.

"What can I help you with?" asked Selena.

"Something, maybe. Where were you last night?"

"Partying with my friend, Chrissie." One last fling Chrissie had said, but Selena had had more final flings than Cher has done farewell tours.

"Just the two of you?"

"Chrissie's boyfriend, Steve, and his friend, Urban. Where did you say you were from?"

"Did you see, or do, anything unusual last night?" Selena's throat tightened, and she felt sweat rise through her pores.

"Like what?"

"Anything you should tell the authorities," said the

86

woman. Selena bit her lip. Urban swore the pills were legal; she wouldn't have touched them if they were dodgy. But the pills were the only thing she'd done last night, except Urban. The woman placed a finger to her left ear, and then smoothed down a single hair that was trying to run from the pony tail.

Selena felt the sweat ooze down her back. "What are you accusing me of?"

"You're the one doing the accusing."

"What? I haven't done anything?"

The woman arched one of her perfectly manicured eyebrows. "Everyone has done something. Our Sumesse cube swarm of sun synchronous satellites detected a powerful sense of guilt from you. We're here to investigate."

There was a knock at the door. The woman's eyes flicked to indicate Selena should answer.

"Hi, Sel," said Phil as Selena opened the door. He kissed her lips and went into the apartment, but stopped at the sight of the visitor. "I didn't know you had company."

The woman ignored Phil. Her finger was pressed to her ear and her eyes were rapidly reading the air. Eventually she turned toward Phil. "And you are?" she asked.

"Phil, Sel's fiancé." Phil held out his hand in greeting.

"I think we have resolution Selena, for now," the woman said as she breezed past Phil's hand, "but we'll be monitoring."

The Bedroom Tax

Susan Howe

I tried to change their minds. I said, "I have to live by myself. I'm not fit to live with other people. Ask my foster mother if you don't believe me."

They said, "You'll lose benefit if you refuse, Nevile. Then you won't be able to pay your rent. Unless you get a job, of course."

They smiled at each other as if I was too stupid to get it. I know what they think of me. I know I'm not like everyone else, but there are much worse people than me. They're on television every day.

I rang Mrs Grace, my nicest foster mother, to try and get her to back me up.

"What do you want, Nevile?" she said, sounding in a hurry, as usual.

"Some women came round and said I had to rent out my spare bedroom or lose my benefit."

"Did you tell them you're not fit to live with other people?" she said.

"Yes, I did."

"Well then, there's nothing to be done. Decent people are losing their homes so you'll just have to do what they say."

"But—"

"I've got to go," she said. "The nappies are boiling over."

She says that every time I ring.

"Okay," I said.

As I was putting the phone down I heard her say, "Oh, Nevile?"

"What?"

"Did they see your collection?"

"No."

"I thought not."

The line went dead.

A letter came that weekend. "Please make the room available for inspection," it said. That meant moving the collection. I made myself some beans on toast and sat looking at it until it got too dark to see it any more.

The next morning I got up early and put on my overalls and wellingtons. It took me all day, shuffling an inch at a time, until it was all in my bedroom, stacked against the wall behind the door. I only spilt a bit and I don't think anyone will spot the hole in the rug.

When the room was empty I scrubbed it from top to bottom and sprayed it with Febreze, which almost hid the smell.

I wondered what sort of person I'd get.

The women came and wrinkled their noses, then shrugged at each other and said, "Beggars can't be choosers."

Two days later Jason turned up. He wheeled his suitcase straight past me into the room and shut the door. When I was in bed he went out and by the time I got up he was back. I heard him moving about for a while and then silence. Every day was the same for three months, until one morning his door was open when I went to the bathroom. There was a strange gurgling sound, so I looked inside. Jason was much too busy with his collection to notice me.

If Mrs Grace thinks I've got problems, she should meet my lodger. I hold my nose when I pass his room and double lock my door at night.

To Test the Senses of Worms
Pauline Masurel

Mr Darwin has been busy today. We are doing our level best to ignore him but this is not easy as he seems intent upon irritating our cerebral ganglia.

At dawn we were unearthed from his garden and deposited upon the billiard table. Since then we have been huffed at, shaken about, and tickled to distraction with a peacock feather. Bright lanterns have been swung above our bodies and a poker heated to dull redness was held mere inches from our segments. Yet not a shred of decomposing leaf nor dewdrop of water have been presented to us since our early morning exhumation.

Then, incremental to these insults, Mr Darwin proceeded to conduct a symphony of random noises in our direction. His wife, who plays most prettily and was taught to depress the keys by Mr Chopin, treated us to her pianoforte skills. Less pleasingly, his children have unleashed the shrieks of a metal whistle and honks of a bassoon to impersonate a flock of geese upon the rampage.

There was nothing we could do to defend ourselves other than bear these depravities in silence. We determined to exhibit no response, hoping that eventually he would desist. After very many hours of experimentation, he has finally done so.

But do not imagine that we shall forget this day, Mr Darwin. There will come a time when you will be among us in the graveyard. We shall be all around you. And also within you. Then we shall set loose our own orchestra of irritations. How will you respond to an assault by the bad-tempered bassoon of our injured sensibilities?

One day, Mr Darwin, your corpse will be nothing more

than rotting meat that is tickled by earthworms. Then let us see how you enjoy being experimented upon by earthworms.

On Taking Measures to Eliminate Fair Play

Kevlin Henney

I'm delighted you could all join this meeting to plan the school fair. As you know, it has been a couple of years since the last one. We feel that the cloud — indeed, storm — hanging over that event has now passed on... as has, sadly, Mrs Pettigrew. Let us remember her for the many years of good work she put into this school and its pupils, and not let one or two episodes mar her memory.

Rather, the increasingly laissez-faire approach of previous years' committees was to blame. The main lesson learnt is the need for greater guidance and supervision.

A certain lack of vigilance in oversight, for example, led to oversights such as the professionally run tattoo stall. At a not inconsiderable expense — particularly challenging without any fund-raising events — I am happy to report that all operations to remove tattoos were completed before our decision to go ahead with this year's fair. We must be on our guard in ensuring that no innocent assumption is left without the strongest presumption of guilt.

Such oversight and stricter guidance applies also to stands being run by parents, especially where the benefit is for the parent body rather than the school or its pupils. Suspicions about the true nature of the *Bare Back Riding* tent were raised only after someone noticed the lack of horses. It had been assumed up until that point that ponies were responsible for the noises.

When this ride was proposed as "being a boon to the swinging community of the school" and that "people would enjoy themselves", it is unlikely Mrs Pettigrew was familiar with the full and colourful range of meanings embraced by the word *swinging*.

We are fortunate that these particular activities were primarily confined to the tent and to adults — and certainly no one younger than the sixth form. On this matter the police were quite thorough.

The clarification over wording is perhaps of even greater importance for the food stalls, whose relaxed aroma, alas, attracted all ages. It proves easy to confuse *hash browns* and *hash brownies*, a distinction that was new to many staff and parents. The revelation that *space cakes* were not the product of some Star Wars themed bake-off offered similar insight and, for some, highlight.

To reinstate the annual fair as a centrepiece of the school's calendar we felt clean decks and new blood were needed to clean the decks of blood... and other bodily fluids. Mrs Pettigrew had been delighted that so many parents who were former pupils of the school had stepped up to the challenge, particularly those she remembered as having a difficult time when they were here. That such formerly disruptive elements would volunteer their time and energy to their alma mater and their own children's time here was, she felt, a vindication of the transformative power of education. It also informed our decision to select you, the new committee, from the congregation of the local church.

Now, moving forward, does anyone have any suggestions?

Handle with Care
Cathy Lennon

She goes with her brother to collect the eggs. He slams out through the screen door that keeps the flies from coming in but doesn't stop the screams from going out. For a moment she flitters her fingertips against the taut mesh before following him. They used to fight over the basket, but Carl is older now and so it sits on the porch, its handle waiting for her. Up ahead he kicks out at the skunk cabbage. He swipes a sleeve across his fringe, damp from the cat-lick. That's what her mother calls it, when she takes the dishrag to their faces, erasing the salt and snot. His cheek is still angry red as a hen's wattle. She trails after him, heart thudding, dew soaking through her shoes.

The sun has set the hen house roof steaming but it isn't hot enough yet to dry the dirt. Way down the hill she glimpses the rusted roof of her father's truck as he takes the bend too fast. She pauses to watch it disappear then skips, her hand outstretched to skim the tickling grass tips. In the dogwood trees birds call to each other and she almost smiles until Carl picks up a stone and hurls it at them. Head down, she keeps him in the corner of her eye. He is inside himself and she knows why, but he should've kept his mouth shut. She takes the picture in her head and transforms it. Her father slaps dust from a rug, lifts it, shakes it, swings it up against the wall and holds it there by its throat-. She falters and the basket nearly slips.

Carl unlatches the door and she follows him inside. The birds flap and squawk. Nostrils full of feather warmth, she wriggles her fingers under straw, searching. It's nearly time for school but she doesn't feel like hurrying. She has lain five eggs gently in the basket when she sees the hen dangling lifeless from his hand. She looks up and quickly away. A twist to his mouth, a baring of teeth that sets a feather to her spine. He isn't looking at her but his body is twitching, like the bird's. She swallows, feels again that scalding dribble between her legs. In her hand the egg's weight lies fragile as her heart. Her fingers curl to cup it safe. They tighten and she senses it against her palm, powerless, waiting, too small and alone to hope for mercy.

The Busker

Eabha Rose

The mud was thick on his boots. It was autumn, late afternoon. People hurried past. He joined the throngs, crossed the park in a straight line like he too had a destination, a plan. It was her time to be here. He knew it. He'd watched her here before, laughing as she jumped on and off the roundabout, spinning in and out of view.

Sitting on the bench, he tried to finish his sandwich before wrapping the remainder in cellophane and shoving it in his pocket. He watched an old man feed the ducks. Funny he thought how some people's lives are so carefully planned. They arrive with food for the ducks, dogs on leads, wrapped up children, books and lunches in tow.

This elusive thing, how she'd felt unreal at times, the memories fragmented , as if they'd been pulled through the mud, crushed like dead leaves. The last time he'd held her she'd been two years old. Her mother had pulled her out of his arms, screaming before he'd staggered across the floor, head spinning from the cocktail of pills and alcohol. He'd spent the next few months in rehab, tried a few times to cut the pain out with a knife before taking up guitar, playing to the passersby and moving from one family to the next.

And then he saw her, long hair swaying, arms outstretched. She ran towards her friends and jumped on the roundabout. He watched her face light up as the wind caught her hair.

He got to his feet, zipped up his coat, dug in his pocket and began to feed the ducks.

Nicotine

Amanda Mason

It wasn't exactly unexpected, in the end.

He'd been in poor health for years, and more or less house bound, with a rota of carers both official and unofficial, calling in, keeping an eye on him.

What with him being on his own.

So when Sarah took the call, when she heard the tone of the woman's voice, she knew what it meant before she heard the words.

She put down the phone and walked back into the kitchen. There were arrangements to be made now, since Jack had no-one else, no-one else to say what should happen to his remains, to deal with the little house and the little bit of money he'd left behind.

She wasn't quite free of him yet.

The kitchen smelt stale and she thought briefly of burnt toast before opening the back door to let the air clear. She wondered that she hadn't noticed it before, in the quiet of the morning as she'd set about some baking.

She went back to work. Creaming butter and sugar for a lemon and lavender cake, wondering how she'd tell Pete and the kids, waiting to feel ... something. She hadn't seen Jack since her mother's funeral; they'd had nothing to say to each other then, and nothing to say in the ten years since.

She worked carefully, cracking the eggs and adding them to the bowl.

Then she paused, irritated, one of the eggs must have been off.

Lifting her wooden spoon, she sniffed cautiously, and dipped a finger into the rich golden mixture.

It tasted fine.

She picked up a lemon, and began to grate the peel.

He hadn't been a bad man, she tried to remind herself, just not a very good one.

And she'd been alright, in the end. She'd managed to hold on until she was eighteen. She'd passed her exams and got out, gone to Uni and never gone back.

She had survived him.

He'd married her mum, a widow, when Sarah was twelve and her one abiding memory of her step father was of his hands, his pudgy, scarred, bruised hands.

Squeezing his wife's bottom as she walked past.

Rolling tobacco into thin cigarettes.

Curling into fists.

The open door wasn't helping. She glanced round the room, something was...

Different.

No.

Missing.

She couldn't smell it; she couldn't smell the lemon at all.

She tried a pinch of dried lavender, crushing the buds between her fingertips.

If only she'd be a good girl, then he wouldn't lose his temper, he'd say, those same hands stroking her hair gently.

His blunt yellow stained fingers.

She couldn't smell the lavender either.

She could only smell...

Him. Stale cigarette smoke and sweet, sweaty nicotine hands, there in her house, on her skin and in her hair.

Clinging to him.

Clinging to her.

As it always had.

Skewed Perspective

Helen Knotts

She woke up horny. Her nipples brushed against the covers and she enjoyed the shiver of pleasure that ran through her. She smiled lasciviously; today was the day.

He woke up tired, brushed his unruly hair out of his eyes and frowned at the clock. He had not remembered that this was the day.

She dressed slowly, smoothing the silk over her skin and watching herself in the mirror as she started to glow. If she'd been a cat she'd have purred. Today, at lunchtime, it would happen.

He threw back a cup of black coffee and pulled a t-shirt over his head. Where the hell were his shoes? Oh yeah, under the chair. He grabbed his keys and slammed the door behind him.

She strolled into town humming to herself. The cherry blossom really did look like 'confetti in her hair'. She felt beautiful. She felt ready.

He worked hard all morning, forcing his mind to bend to the day's problems. Something gnawed at the back of his memory. At around 11.30 he started to feel hungry. Shit! Lunch!

She sat at a table in the garden, it would be a shame to waste such a gorgeous day. A warm breeze shifted her hair against her ear and put her in mind of a whispering lover. She crossed her legs and pressed her thighs together as the need in her rose.

He raced out of the office. He couldn't be late. This was it. This was the day when the waiting would finally be over. All the work and effort would be worthwhile. Damn this traffic.

Late! How could he be late? She started to worry, maybe he didn't feel the same way. But somehow, she wasn't as upset as she should be. After all, had it been much more than just great sex?

His hand punched the steering wheel as he screamed at jaded drivers to hurry up, to get out of his way. She was waiting. The one. Everything was waiting for him. He dared to let his spirits rise as he rubbed his thumb against the ring box in his pocket. The culmination of all his hopes and dreams was mere streets away.

Still not here. She didn't want to look foolish. Perhaps a shopping spree would salvage the day. Her sense of perspective now skewed, she placed her napkin neatly on the table and walked away.

Bread

Ingrid Jendrzejewski

The baker recoiled at the taste of the handshake. The proffered hand smacked of crystallised sweat with a hint of grime - nothing like the yeasty, slightly sweet dough into which he longed to bury his fingers. Only, he wasn't going to be doing much kneading anymore, precisely because he was shaking hands with persons like this.

The baker glanced nervously at the man in a fashionable suit and a tasteful tie. If the businessman had noticed the baker's less graceful termination of the handshake, he didn't give any indication. The deal had been made; ducks were in a row. There was no need to say anything more. Parting pleasantries were exchanged, and the baker held the mildly brackish door open for the businessman. Once alone, he collapsed in a chair and sighed, resting his bland forehead in his hands.

The merger was a great step forward. The baker's products would reach more mouths than ever before, and the money was, he had to admit, fantastic. There was no doubt that he was doing the right thing by his family. And yet....

The baker looked around his humble office, carefully outfitted with taste-neutral furniture and fixtures. He'd miss this place. The new factory was much larger, and almost certainly not designed with someone like him in mind.

The fact was that he had been born with taste-sensitive hands. It ran in the family. He came from a long line of men who were only suited for very specific lines of work: unfortunately, most of the world is ambivalent about the taste of objects around them. For years, baking offered some degree of respite; with one's hands buried in the wholesome, slightly earthy combination of sugar, flour, water and yeast, one could almost forget the perils of the rest of the world - the metallic bite of doorknobs, the tart kick of grimy light switches, even the acrid bitterness of hand-soap.

That life was all over now, he feared. No longer would he be kneading dough by hand, then lovingly caressing the freshly-baked loaves as he wrapped them up for market. Machines would take care of all that now, machines he imagined would taste acerbic, bitter and sharp, seasoned only by the spicy tang of cash.

The Notes Play On

Shirley Golden

The notes play on in his head and heart, as do the jeers of the mob, and his son's pleas. Wade stares across the surface sand, white with heat. The land smells of a violin scratch, like his grandpa used to create every Sunday after church.

The kid's shadow falls shy of shading Wade's head. He rubs the stubble on his chin and squats.

'It ain't worth it, old-timer. Tell me where you buried it, and this'll be over.'

Wade tries to tally words to meaning but they chime same as bells for weddings or funerals alike.

The kid had forced the stagecoach to stop, wielding a Colt and shooting the driver. He ripped open the first sack, and finding nothing but letters inside, set it alight. Wade snatched the other bag and ran, his windpipe fizzing, topping his chest with pain.

'Tell me where it is, an' spare us both a deal of trouble. Can't be far.'

'There ain't nothin' of value for you.' Wade feels the sting of saliva in the cracks along his lips.

'Then why you hide it, eh?'

Wade shifts as far as the ropes will allow. He hears the scurry of a jack rabbit, kicking up a mustard trail. The bullet in his knee burns brighter than the sun. His hat is out of reach, speared with jumping cholla. Blood hangs in his throat and tastes of metal shavings. The letter he bears is as heavy as the scent of his daughter's perfume on the day of the funeral. In the shrub, the chuparosa attract humming birds. Wade listens for the whirr rising from their wings to his senses.

The kid unbuttons his pants, and takes a piss against a

cactus. Droplets hiss and hit the earth, golden to black.

Wade never thought his life would end in this bid to set the world to rights; it was a crusade not even his wife understood.

He hums his grandpa's tune. He'll be seeing him soon, of that he's sure.

'Last chance, old-timer,' the kid says.

'It's just letters.'

'It ain't just letters – not even a fool'd waste his life for that.'

***

Wade's son was accused of rustling old Haskell's horses, and they'd waited on the promised pardon; it arrived after the lynch mob.

He should explain how some folk can be saved by the most unlikely things but the words are stuck somewhere between heart and throat.

***

The kid searches, until he finds the sack and rips it open; letters spew out. Page after page flutter and reach a crescendo above the haze. He sinks to his knees. 'Crazy old-timer.'

He kicks loose sand over the body, says a prayer, and picks up Wade's hat.

A tune knocks around his head, and he's unsure from where it came, but it floats outwards into the scrub and joins the whirr of humming bird wings.

The Five Senses

Caroline Worsley

Peter opened his book, picked up his pencil and copied the title from the board, 'The Five Senses'. He always tried to listen in class but the remembering bit of him didn't seem to work very well.

'Senses,' he thought. Well there was a 'sense of humour', because Dad was always saying Mum hadn't got one when she didn't laugh at his jokes. Peter was pleased he'd made a start. What next?

The other day, when they went for a walk in the woods and didn't know how to get back to the car, his brother David had found the way. Mum said he must have a good 'sense of direction'.

Peter looked round the room. Some of his class-mates were busy writing, some rubbing out, some drawing patterns down the side of the page, some staring into space. The third sense came to him. 'She has such a sense of purpose, on her way to nowhere.' Mum said this about Nanny Ann when she saw her going to the shops where she never ever bought anything. Number three.

Sounds of music came from the hall. It reminded him of the party at New Year. When Auntie Vera watched his Mum and Dad dancing she laughed so much she nearly cried. 'Jack, you've no sense of rhythm,' she'd spluttered.

Peter knew there was a film called 'Sixth Sense', but his teacher, Mrs Morris, only wanted five. He could feel her getting close to him as she walked slowly round the room, scanning her pupils' work as she passed by. She stopped at Peter's table and read.

1. Mum dusnt get dads joks. but there not even very funy.
2. Dav fownd the car were we left it

3.Nannyann dusnt go shoping
4.Dad dansed at new yer
5.

Peter looked up anxiously at Mrs Morris. She raised her eyes towards the ceiling. She clenched her fist and shook it in mock rage. 'Peter Manley. Sometimes I just wish I could knock come sense into you!'

His face brightened. 'Miss,' he said hopefully, 'is that a clue to number five?'

Vinegar

T Upchurch

— Yow's a weird lookin' frog.

— Wot?

— Yow's a weird lookin' frog, no good tellin' me yow in't, because yow is a weird lookin' frog.

— I in't.

He's kickin' stones and we're waitin'. The sun burns our foreheads and the backs of our necks. The dust he kicks up sticks to our sweat.

— And yow stink.

— I dun't.

— Yow stinks like yaw mum.

— She dun't.

— She duz.

His mum comes first, chewin' on somethin'. She dun't speak, just opens the door and he gets in. She leans out the window.

— Yaw mum comin'?

— Yeh.

She pulls her head back in, but my mum dun't come. She dun't drive off neither, so they just sit there. I kick some dust. He watches me out the window.

She gives him a bag. It crackles when he opens it, and we all smell vinegar. He pulls out a great big, golden crisp and puts it in his mouth. It crunches, all muffled by his face, and the vinegar gets stronger. There's salt and grease on his fingers and he licks them. My mouth fills up with spit and my stomach roars.

He says somethin' I dun't hear. She nods. He sticks his head out.

— Yow wan' a come in?

I nod.

— Mah mum'll call yaw mum.

I grin. I'm runnin' to the door to open it because in there, I'll have a crisp on my tongue all the way home. I'm goin' to press it up against the roof o' my mouth till it cracks an' the vinegar fills my nose. When I swallow, I'm gonna feel it go down, and I'll be shiverin' for another. He'll give it me too. He's nasty but he shares.

I'm at the door when our car turns up, spinnin' dust into clouds. I stand still.

— That yaw mum?

— No.

My tongue is nearly hurtin': I want my crisp.

My mum gets out the car and speaks to his mum. They're smilin'. From where I'm standin', I can see right down into his bag. It's all silver foil and the crisps are curled around each other like in a nest. The top one's a folded one with a bubble in it, and I can see the salt sparklin'.

My mum calls 'bye, then pulls me over to our car. I get in because I have to, and she turns the key. She in't brought crisps for me, so my belly rumbles away while my nose tries to forget what just happened. We stare at the road while she drives and after a minute I can't smell vinegar any more — just salt and dust and sweat.

My ears can still hear him saying my mum stinks and I think, it's true. She does.

Hotdogs

Dixon Barker

Unless it was winter, George always mowed the grass first. He'd aim to cut tight to an invisible fence-line, but would inevitably slip over a little into the neighbour's plot. When he was finished he'd turn on the shower, afterwards he'd change his shirt. He'd heat the water on the stove beforehand and ask his son, Albert, to put the hotdogs in the pan. They didn't need to be taken out of their packet you just popped them in and watched them boil. Sometimes he'd dare Albert to try and take them out when they were done. "Don't play with fire! Either of you," Albert's Mum would warn from the sitting room. Albert wasn't stupid, he was afraid of being caught and concerned about the pain that would follow. His Dad would always wink at him and shout, "Only joking," then fish out the packet with own his broad fingers, undaunted. He was good with the heat and he was good with his hands. Sometimes, when Albert went to bed he'd hear them both through the stud wall; his mum telling his dad, "You're so good with your hands, George." Sometimes - when his Mum wasn't around - Albert would catch the woman from next-door also telling his Dad, "Oh, George, you are good with your hands," and she'd wink. This would make Albert wonder, was his Dad was at all like him? Scared to play with fire; afraid of being caught and concerned about the pain that would follow.

All the Rage

Ian Shine

When my skin changed, revealing symmetrical beads of blushes over my plain white background, I knew that polka dot was about to come back into fashion.

The same had happened last season, when floral prints had been all the rage, and the year before with check.

"Oh my God, I love what you've done to yourself this time," my doctor said. "Where did you get the idea?"

"I don't know. It just came to me."

"Well I'll definitely take it. Just let me…"

She took off all her clothes and stood in front of me.

"You'll have to come over at the weekend, if you're free. My friends will absolutely love this."

She came right up next to me and rubbed her body against mine. After a couple of minutes she looked at herself in the mirror, smiled, and put her clothes back on.

I went over that weekend, as I had for the past two years and would for the next five, when my skin would slip from stripes to swirls to baggy to faded to gold. I saw other doctors too, and all their friends. I was the most popular I'd ever been.

But then one year everything vanished, and I just turned plain white. Even my smudges of chest hair fell out, and when I went to see the doctor to ask her what was going on, she kept her clothes on and told me to stop wasting her time.

I screamed and begged for her to touch me, but she said she could either ask me to leave again or press the buzzer and have me escorted out.

In the surgery waiting room I picked up a couple of women's glossies and ran out. At home I learnt that rips and rags were going to be in this season, so I took a knife to my knees and chest and stumbled back to the doctor. She sent me straight to A&E and said she'd pop over to see me later. She'd bring her friends if that was alright.

The Sixth Generation

Jonathan Pinnock

The Principal looked at Mr Arbuthnot and raised an eyebrow.

'Yes?' she said.

Arbuthnot shuffled in his chair, unsure where to start. 'Well, it's like this,' he said. 'You know we've always had a rule about the use of hand-held devices in class?'

'Yes,' said the Principal.

'Well, we've got a bit of a problem. Since all this 6G business has started, we're having trouble spotting them. They're almost invisible now.'

'Yes.'

'And what's worse, it's not just Google glasses and nano earbuds and whatnot. The kids have got all their senses wired up now. They've got gizmos up their noses and under their tongues, touch pads on their fingers, even – ' Arbuthnot paused, feeling the colour rise in his cheeks.

'Yes?'

'Even ... they've even got sensors in their undergarments,' he said, his voice dropping to a whisper. 'It's ... unseemly.'

'Yes,' said the Principal, nodding.

'You don't know what they're getting up to. I've heard talk of – what do they call them – vorgies? Going on right under our noses. In class. Without us even knowing!' He paused to take out his handkerchief and wipe sweat from his brow. 'Madam – '

'Yes?'

'Madam, I know you probably think I'm just an old fogey who's out of touch with all this modern stuff, but I'm just thinking about the kids. Virtually fumbling and groping each other while we're trying to get them to understand Pythagoras, caressing each other's taut virtual flesh while we're discussing irregular transitive verbs, wrapping their virtual tongues around each other while we ... I mean, where is it all going to end?'

'Yes...' said the Principal, her eyes glazing over.

'You do understand what I'm saying?' said Arbuthnot.

But the Principal was in a world of her own. 'Yes,' she said, her voice getting louder, 'Yes ... yes ... yes ...'

Where Memories Live
Jennifer Harvey

Mother comes to help.

She folds the corners of my bed sheets with a satisfied smile. She is home again, at last.

"Rest up" she says.

"It's as good as a cure" I reply.

And she pats my head and nods, glad that I still remember.

I listen as she clatters round the kitchen.

Cleaning out the oven, she finds a baking tray, black and encrusted. I know finding it just made her nose crease.

She does not see the patina of feasts, some remembered, most forgotten. She does not hear the wine soaked nights of laughter and indulgence. Does not smell the lust scented smoke of hand rolled cigarettes.

All she sees is the residue of a life not so well lived.

I hear her tut, then the rattle of the bin as she kicks the pedal.

"No, leave it!" I cry

But she has drowned me out with a boiling kettle.

*

I wake to see a mug on the bedside table, the tea gone cold.

The whole house smells like a pine forest after a shower of summer rain, a smell that transports me, in a fevered daze, to an afternoon before all this.

She scoured the house that day too. From top to bottom.

And though I was small, I understood she needed to erase the traces of him, the pieces of him that had gathered in every nook and cranny.

114

She washed skirting boards, dusted window ledges, siphoned detritus from between sofa cushions.

As if he existed there still, in these places which are largely unseen and unnoticed.

"What is it you are trying to erase?" I wondered. "The whole of your past? Or just him?"

But I noticed the soil beneath her fingernails. The way she left it there for days, never taking a brush to it.

The last connection she had to him, the one you would imagine she would not want to keep, because who wants the sound of that thud on a casket resonating in their fingertips, their heart?

"I made some soup. You think you can take some?"

"As long as it's not oxtail."

We smile at one another, remembering the whining child I once was. The one that squirmed and gagged at the mere mention of it.

"Vegetable" she says "Got to keep your strength up."

I surprise her. Raise myself up from the bed and into the kitchen where the table is not set.

She jumps a little when she sees me standing there, my presence already ghostly, before setting two places.

We sit facing one another, sipping soup, both of us knowing the moment is a memory only she will carry forward.

Cherished

Kay Beer

These hands that touch me... which have the strength to bend copper pipe at a 45 degree angle, yet gentle enough to hold our daughters tiny fingers and guide her faltering steps across the polished beech wood floor.

Un-tanned, broad spans of palms act as shovels to scoop up Lego bricks, discarded by our son. Large bright coloured bricks that earlier in the day you lay on the floor to build, with care into towers. Only to have them smashed by a single swipe of his hand and as you mockingly complain, 'Oh no!' Peals of laughter ring out as he squeals with glee, 'Again, again.'

You dislike public displays of affection they're not your style. Surrounded by ice cream sundaes and pink roses that same hand trembled as you dipped to one knee to propose. Just for a laugh those nimble fingers snapped the engagement ring box shut, with such a crack I jumped off my seat, before I had time to say yes.

At our engagement party we were fooling about, you picked up the sherry trifle, turned it upside down and span the glass bowl round my head. The room erupted; our guests couldn't contain their laughter as dribs of jelly and drabs of custard slopped down my arms. Afterwards you teased out tinned pineapple chunks and cubed lumps of pear as you showered the mess from my hair.

When there's a storm brewing and I resemble a small boat tied to a forgotten mooring, you stroke my arm. Your caress calms me, steadies my nerves. These dependable hands that hold me with adulation and after we've made love those same hands that hold our bull mastiff on a tethered lead for her morning walk round the village common.

When I'm nervous you place your hand, in the small of my back, guide me to safety. The same soft fingertips with trimmed nails that before you vacate our crumpled warm bed know how and where to plunder me with a lightness of touch which draws such sweet music. Unable to resist, my body twitches to your love tap, bringing forth moans of joy before I end with a big bang that ensnares me in ecstasy.

At the end of a tough day when my back aches your experienced fingers massage liniment to dislodge tight knots. This deep kneading action and pungent menthol odour, eases my tension. Your hands work their magic, as balm for my soul.

Once the children sleep, cradled in your arms I rest, the full length of our bodies touch, skin against skin, as your tenderness traces a never ending pattern across and down my bare back.

And after we talk through the days events, as I drift off to sleep you enfold your fingers through mine, wrapping each finger, one between the other you cup my hand in yours, and press our enclosed hand together, against your heart. These unwritten rules of your hands, these coded messages fill me with desire.

A Sticky End

Cath Barton

Kev said I was making it up.

"Can't you smell her?" I said.

He said he could only smell popcorn, that all cinemas smelled of popcorn and what was peculiar about that?

"Nothing," I said, "except that the smell of popcorn is a cover."

He said I was a fantasist and I said that was rich coming from him, being as his favourite film was 'Lord of the Rings'.

I don't how I dared, but one day I snapped off a couple of her candy-pink fingernails as she handed me our tickets. I passed one to Kev to suck during the film.

"This is nice," he said, "strawberry-flavoured. I didn't know they sold those."

I told him they didn't and what it really was, and he started yelling at me, but the people behind us were shushing so he had to wait till the end of the film to find out the truth.

"It wasn't really her fingernail, it couldn't have been," he said as we stood outside waiting for her to lock up.

I said it was and that he would see, when she appeared, that two of her nails were broken.

"You're sick in the head," he said, when he saw what I said was true.

I told Kev I couldn't go to the cinema the next week, said I didn't like the films. But I went one day without him so I could enjoy looking at her without his wisecrack remarks. I loved her shiny black liquorice curls. When I got near the front of the queue she came out from behind her counter and there was a waft of aniseed. It made me feel quite woozy.

Summer was coming and the aromas in the cinema were

getting sweeter and stronger. Kev said the popcorn must be coming in different flavours, but as she gave me our tickets I got the aniseed scent from her hair again. I didn't say anything to Kev, just handed him his treat during the film.

It got hotter and hotter and the woman in the box office was looking rather dishevelled. Kev said she was letting herself go and I said I didn't think she had any choice in the matter, being what she was. I could see her hands getting limp as she handed over the tickets, and all her nails were broken now. It made me sad to see what was becoming of her, to smell her in her decline.

One day there was a sign on the cinema door: Vacancy for box-office assistant. People said she must have had a better offer, but of course I knew she'd come to a sticky end. Kev said I watched too many films. But I knew he was as disappointed as I was when the new woman started and we were back eating boring old popcorn. I think he missed the edible woman as much as I did, though, being Kev, he was never going to admit it.

Strangers
L. D. Lapinski

Below the table, the two men's legs both reached out towards the opposite seat, politely avoiding kicking and shoe-shuffling. It was with a forced, nonchalant sniff that the younger man leaned his right leg slightly to make contact with the heavy denim covering that of the man opposite. There was a twitch of surprise from the unexpected contact, then the businessman's muscle relaxed, allowing the weight of the first man's limb to rest, leaning. The youth's eyes continued to stare out of the window, and the suit's fingers still traced the touchpad on his laptop.

A slight clearing of the throat from the older man, and the youth felt his leaning leg become trapped in an embrace as the stranger's left leg leaned to put weight on top of his, sandwiching it. The youth, adjusting his earphones, completed the pattern by shifting his weight and running his left leg slightly along the material of the expensive suit trousers, pulling slightly at the fabric before settling, knee touching shin.

The two men carried on evading eye contact, one texting, one typing in denial of the slightly moving, touching, limbs beneath eye contact. The only clue that either of them was aware of their lower body was the tremor of the businessman's hands and the icy grey veil that had dropped over the eyes of the silent youth.

The train rattled north.

Cider and Simnel

Nuala Ní Chonchúir

My mother looks undone, slumped in an ancient deck chair by the back door. She sits, hands a-dangle above a mug of homemade cider, as if some creature might swoop down and steal it away. She has probably sat here all day.

Squinting up at me with one languid eye, the other closed, she says, 'I hope, Helen, you're not expecting tea. There's nothing reasonable to eat.'

'Mam,' I say, 'this is Cal.'

My mother raises a hand as if the uncharacteristic spring heat does away with the need for words.

'We ate in town,' Cal offers.

'Of course you did,' my mother says. 'Have a sup of cider, Cal. Helen, get glasses.'

I go to the kitchen and pluck two cups from the draining board; they are, of course, hennaed with tannin but Cal won't mind. I come out the back door and watch the sun drift west. I heave the demi-john of cider from the old sink, where it steeps in cold water, and pour.

'I made a simnel cake,' my mother says. 'And I fired Patsy.'

'What did she take this time?' I ask.

'The portrait of your father. Not the ugly one.'

'You should have let her have it.'

'I did. But I got rid of her, too.'

The cider is flat, but cool and welcome slipping down my throat. Cal is perched on the back step and I sit beside him. The heat that radiates from his body brings back our morning in my bed: the slick, fierce weight of him on top of me, his soft grunts and smiles.

My mother sips and belches quietly between each

121

draught. 'The apples are sweeter since your father died,' she says.

'You might be right,' I answer, but my mind is adrift, wondering if the ferocity of new love can ever last. If Cal and I stay together, will I always want to coil up on his chest after sex? Will I still relish the scatter of hair in the small of his back that I stroke like a pet while he sleeps? And will he hold me all night, pursuing me across the sheets when I try to ease away? I take Cal's hand in mine and kiss each knuckle in turn; he grins and pucks me gently with his side.

'Cake,' my mother says, 'we must have cake with our cider.' She rocks herself out of the deck chair in a series of swings and snarls and goes to the kitchen. She returns with the simnel cake on a platter, its top a blaze of marzipan dotted with sugar-shelled eggs. Standing over Cal and me, she examines us. 'You look right together,' she says. 'Bless your youth. Bless your future. Eat this cake and drink this cider.'

So we do. And we sit, the three of us, and talk of love and death and birth, and so much more besides, until the April sun drops behind the orchard and is gone.

National Flash-Fiction Day 2014 Micro-Fiction Competition Winners:

First Place

Never Let Me Go
Cathy Lennon

First it was cartons and tins on the worktops, then newspapers on the stairs. Each window-sill sparkled with tin foil. He made me a necklace of ring-pulls and bottle tops. Like swans we perched on our bundles of rags and flattened boxes, smoothing the creases from wrappers. The hallway was Manhattan, a canyon of towering piles. Across the no man's land in our bedroom our fingertips would touch, until one day they couldn't anymore. From the other side, perplexed, he watched the tears slide down my face. He threw me two empty film canisters to catch them in.

Second Place

Night-time Knitting
Roz Mascall

A gorilla is living in my cupboard. Every night, he swaggers onto my bed and waits for me to wake-up. I pretend to be asleep but hear his knitting needles clicking together. He is making a very long scarf for me. Squinting at him from under my blanket, I see his huge hairy hands scratch his scalp in disappointment. He looks sad. A pang of guilt hits me. I sit up and he hands me a ball of pink wool. His watery eyes meet my gaze. He is lonely. We lean against each other and knit until sunrise.

Third Place

If Kissed by a Dragon Fish
Tania Hershman

If kissed by a dragonfish, do not bite. If kissed by a dragonfish, make sure you are sitting. Do not worry during the kiss, before the kiss, or after. Do not worry about a scale or two between your teeth. The dragonfish's skin is armoured but its heart beats loud and soft. You will not forget the kiss. You will not forget the coolness of the dragonfish's breath inside your lungs. You will look down through the floor of glass and see nothing, swimming. You will part, like an ocean, and on your sea bed you will pearl.

Highly Commended

Dare
Simon Sylvester

Every day that summer, we played Dare. On hot afternoons we escaped the sun by hiding in the fort. We ate apples and counted pips and swapped secrets. We sat close, damp with sweat, bare skin sticking. She traced her fingers up my leg. Her fingertips whispered inside my thigh, and my breath caught in my throat.

She always chickened out. I taunted her, urging her higher, but she always chickened out before me.

When that summer was finished, we went back to school. We don't really talk any more.

I heard she started playing Dare with boys.

Sintra
Parineeta Singh

I have followed you to this small town. I have walked the same cobblestones that you once trod on. I have stood on those hilltops in the mist you spoke of. I have felt it as smoke in my throat. The air I now exhale was the air you once breathed in. But this is not love; it is nowhere close to it. Love was the time when I put my ear to the flagstones listening for your footfall.

The Star, Falling
Morgan Downie

When his eyes grew so bad that he could no longer see the horizon he built an artificial one in his garden. Afterwards he persisted in a stubborn refusal to cross it in case he should fall off the edge of the world. Asked, on reflection, if he had realised his intention as a younger man, to live the brief and fiery life of a meteor, he looked out across the universe of his garden, to the wife he still loved indescribably and said, 'I am a meteor, just moving very, very slowly.'

The Sponge Diver
Danielle McLaughlin

They knew each other a month when he told her about his Greek grandfather who, as a young man, had been a sponge diver. She closed her eyes, saw a figure – lithe, tanned – dive naked from a boat in the blue Aegean. He surfaced, water glittering silver on his skin, as if a shoal of tiny fish had followed him.

Opening her eyes, she noticed how her lover was most unlike a sponge diver.

After it ended, she bought a sea sponge, yellow and pocked. She sat it on her desk at work, and thought about his grandfather.

Peppermint

Jennifer Harvey

Afterwards, he thought about the gum stuck underneath the desk. It would still be there.

Every morning he watched as she slipped a finger in her mouth and prised it out, acting coy, though he knew she was aware of him.

Once, she'd looked him in the eye, stretched the gum between her teeth and let it snap, like a flirtatious wink.

He slid his fingers under the rim. It was still there.

Picking it loose, he popped it in his mouth.

It was fragrant, peppermint fresh. A taste of her he could keep and roll across his tongue.

The Invisible Girl

Karl A Russell

It should have been an accident, Mel always thought. Something sciencey and catastrophic. Experimental bombs, or maybe the bite of an irradiated marmoset. That's how it used to happen in the comics anyway; A good dose of cosmic waves transformed you.

And everyone loved you.

Even the villains.

But there were no sciencey accidents in the real world. All it took to make Mel invisible was a split lip, or a black eye, or a few raised voices on a Saturday night, just after chucking out time.

And then, for just a little while, no-one could see her.

4am
Angi Holden

I open the bedroom curtains.

Dawn seeps across the horizon. The long grass beneath the hive glistens with dew. Hand-trimming takes patience; this summer I've neglected the garden.

I straighten the sheet across your chest. The air cradles the sour milk and vinegar scent of the sickroom.

Downstairs, I fumble with the lock, step into the morning. My slippers absorb the damp. No matter, I have a task to perform. Before I call the doctor, your sister, our son.

I walk down the path, your black crepe bowtie dangling from my hand. There is news I must tell the bees.

Author List

We don't have enough room in a volume such as this to list a full biography for all of our authors, and anyway, we don't have to when they have all already done the job for us on their blogs and websites.

So, below, please find a list of the places on the World-Wide Web where you can follow up the authors from this anthology. Please read their other work, buy their books, and generally support them. That way they can continue to bring you wonderful stories like the ones you've just read.

Christopher Allsop www.callsop.com
Dixon Barker dixonbarkerisalive.blogspot.co.uk
Rhys Barter @rhysbart
Cath Barton www.blipfoto.com/Cathaber
Kay Beer 1lovelife.blogspot.co.uk
A. Joseph Black www.ajosephblack.com/ @Gram_is_God_TB
Cath Bore www.cathbore.com
Cathy Bryant cathybryant.co.uk
Ed Broom freston.net/blog / @edbroom
Andy Cashmore andycashmore.wordpress.com / @AndyJCash
Nuala Ní Chonchúir nualanichonchuir.com
James Coates @Brev_
Moira Conway moiraconway.wordpress.com
David Coss dpcoss@gmail.com
Morgan Downie morgandownie.com
Marie Gethins @MarieGethins
Shirley Golden www.shirleygolden.net
Jennifer Harvey www.jenharvey.net
Kevlin Henney asemantic.net
Tania Hershman taniahershman.com
Sarah Hilary sarah-crawl-space.blogspot.co.uk
Angi Holden @josephsyard
Jenny Holden www.evewhite.co.uk/authors/jenny-holden/
Richard Holt bigstorysmall.com
Susan Howe howesue.wordpress.com
Ingrid Jendrzejewski www.ingridj.com

Andy Jenkinson   www.andyjenkinson.com
Davina Jones   @davinahjones
Calum Kerr   www.calumkerr.co.uk
John F King   www.johnkinginternational.eu
Helen Knotts   @HelenKnotts
L. D. Lapinski   @ldlapinski / www.ldlapinski.com
Andy Lavender   www.alavenderwrites.com
Emmaleene Leahy   emmaleene.wordpress.com.
Cathy Lennon   @clenpen
Danielle McLaughlin   @DanniLmc
Nigel McLoughlin   www.nigelmcloughlin.co.uk
Amy Mackelden   www.clarissaexplainsfuckall.com / @july2061
Roz Mascall   www.rozmascall.co.uk
Amanda Mason   @amandajanemason
Pauline Masurel   www.unfurling.net / @unfurlingnet
E.L. Norry   Marks533@gmail.com
Sonya Oldwin   about.me/sonya.oldwin
Sal Page   sal-cobbledtogether.blogspot.co.uk
Cassandra Parkin   www.cassandraparkin.wordpress.com
Nik Perring   nikperring.com / @nikperring
Jonathan Pinnock   www.jonathanpinnock.com
Pam Plumb   pamjplumb.wordpress.com
Tino Prinzi   @tinoprinzi
Angela Readman   @angelreadman
Jane Roberts   janeehroberts.wordpress.com
Eabha Rose   theatreofwords.blogspot.ie
Miranda Roszkowski   roszkodysseus.wordpress.com /
@miranda_roszko
Karl A Russell   @Karl_A_Russell
Jeanette Sheppard   @InkLinked
Ian Shine   ianshinejournalism.blogspot.co.uk / @ianshine
Selina SIAK Chin Yoke   chinyoke.wordpress.com.
Diane Simmons   @scooterwriter
Parineeta Singh
Tim Stevenson   timjstevenson.com
Simon Sylvester   www.simonsylvester.wordpress.com
Michael Marshall Smith   www.michaelmarshallsmith.com
Becky Tipper   www.thebookflea.com
T Upchurch   www.traceyupchurch.com
Colin Watts   www.colinwatts.net
Adam J Wolstenholme   adamjwolstenholme.blogspot.co.uk
Caroline Worsley
Debbie Young   www.authordebbieyoung.com

Acknowledgements etc.

As usual when creating a book like this, we have a roster of appreciation to go through.

Thanks, of course, to all the writers who submitted both to this anthology and our earlier competition. You provided the words, we just arranged them on a page.

It could never have happened without Angela Readman— with whose help all the stories were selected—and Amy Mackelden who formatted the manuscript and chose the elegant ordering of the pieces.

Thanks also to the prominent writers who donated flashes to the collection.

Thanks to Tim Stevenson, for playing keyboards.

And, of course, thanks to my wife and boy for their constant support and teasing.

However, final thanks must go to you, the reader, for picking up a copy of this book and delving inside. We do all of this for you, and we thank you.

Calum Kerr
Director of NFFD

Sarah Hilary's *A Shanty for Sawdust and Cotton* won the SENSE Creative Award in 2010. SENSE is the UK's leading deaf-blind charity; please consider donating: www.sense.org.uk

Angela Readman was also one of the judges of the NFFD competition. Her story collection *Don't Try this at This Home* will be published by & Other Stories.

Also Available from
National Flash-Fiction Day

Jawbreakers
(NFFD 2012)

A collection of flash- and micro-fictions gathered together by National Flash-Fiction Day 2012. Includes stories from Ian Rankin, Vanessa Gebbie, Jenn Ashworth, Tania Hershman, David Gaffney, Trevor Byrne, Jen Campbell, Jonathan Pinnock, Calum Kerr, Valerie O'Riordan and many more. 62 tales spanning different genres, styles and themes, but all beautifully crafted in just a few well-chosen words.

Scraps
(NFFD 2013)

Scraps is the second anthology from National Flash-Fiction Day. It features more than seventy huge tales told in only a few words.

All of the stories in this collection have been inspired by other works of art: paintings, sculptures, TV programmes, films, music and more. As a result they are imbued with something of the original, but then take off into new and often surprising directions.

Funny, sad, exciting, intriguing, experimental and traditional, Scraps is a snapshot of the best in contemporary flash fiction.

Other books from **Gumbo Press**:
www.gumbopress.co.uk

The Book of Small Changes
by Tim Stevenson

This collection takes its inspiration from the Chinese I Ching: where the sea mourns for those it has lost, encyclopaedia salesmen weave their accidental magic, and the only true gift for a king is the silence of snow.

Enough by Valerie O'Riordan

Fake mermaids and conjoined twins, Johannes Gutenberg, airplane sex, anti-terrorism agricultural advice, Bluebeard and more.
Ten flash-fictions.

Threshold by David Hartley

Threshold explores the surreal and the strange through thirteen flash-fictions which take us from a neighbour's garden, out into space, and even as far as Preston. But which Preston?

Undead at Heart by Calum Kerr

War of the Worlds meets *The Walking Dead* in this novel from Calum Kerr, author of *31* and *Braking Distance*

The World in a Flash: How to Write Flash Fiction by Calum Kerr

A guide for beginners and experienced writers alike to give you insight into the world of flash-fiction. Chapters focus on a range of aspects, with exercises for you to try.

The 2014 Flash365 Collections
by Calum Kerr

Apocalypse
It's the end of the world as we know it.
Fire is raining from the sky, monsters are rising from the deep., and the human race is caught in the middle.

The Audacious Adventuress
Our intrepid heroine, Lucy Burkhampton, is orphaned and swindled by her evil nemesis, Lord Diehardt. She must seek a way to prove her right to her family's wealth, to defeat her enemy, and more than anything, to stay alive.

The Grandmaster
Unrelated strangers are being murdered in a brutal fashion. Now it's up to crime-scene cleaner Mike Chambers, with the help of the police, in the form of his friend, DC James Worth, to track down the killer and stop the trail of carnage.

Lunch Hour
One office. Many lives. It is that time of day: the time for poorly-filled, pre-packaged sandwiches; the time to run errands you won't have enough time for; the time to fall in love, to kill or be killed, to take advice from an alien. It's the Lunch Hour.

Made in the USA
Middletown, DE
06 September 2017